She was still bent over him, reaching for something next to the bed, then to his face which she touched with a soft, cool cloth. Now she touched along his neck; and, gently drawing back the covers, began dabbing something onto his body. It was painful, but the feeling of being cared for outweighed the pain. She bent closer to him and a lock of her hair fell into his eyes. Even in his pain Slocum felt a stirring . . .

# OTHER BOOKS BY JAKE LOGAN

# JAKE LOGAN

# THE SUNSHINE BASIN WAR

BERKLEY BOOKS, NEW YORK

THE SUNSHINE BASIN WAR

A Berkley Book/published by arrangement with
the author

PRINTING HISTORY
Berkley edition/September 1985

ISBN: 0-425-08087-0

A BERKLEY BOOK ® TM 757,375
Berkley Books are published by Berkley Publishing Group,
200 Madison Avenue, New York, NY 10016.
The name "BERKLEY" and the stylized "B" with design are
trademarks belonging to Berkley Publishing Corporation.

PRINTED IN THE UNITED STATES OF AMERICA

# 1

In the clean mountain air the spotted pony picked its way haltingly down the thin, rocky trail, its hind foot caught in a piece of rotted timber which it had stepped through when its rider had been shot out of the saddle. Alongside the empty saddle the stock of a Winchester rifle protruded from its scabbard, bobbing with each step taken by the horse, tantalizingly out of reach of the man who was being dragged along, his foot fouled in the hackamore rope that was coiled at the side of the pommel.

The man was almost naked, his clothes torn from his bruised and bloody body as he was pulled along the rough, cutting trail. Yet he still gripped the horse's reins in one hand, the Colt Peacemaker in the other.

Now, as the little bronc stopped to chomp at a

sparse clump of grass along the side of the trail, the man switched the Colt to his hand that was holding the reins and again tried to reach up to grab the stirrup and lift himself, but his fingers fell inches short. He dropped back to his prone position, not cursing, refusing to curse in his frustration, for he knew he needed every drop of energy to survive.

Yet John Slocum's attention was still keen, keen beyond his exhaustion and pain, for in the next instant his eye caught the mountain jay breaking from the clump of pine near the timberline above him. In the crack of the rifle shot that echoed all the way down the long, wide valley his own hand-gun bucked as he pulled the trigger, almost lapping the bushwhacker's bullet. And he fired again. But there was no second rifle shot. There was silence.

Had he got the son of a bitch? There was no way of knowing as the startled bronc yanked him farther down the trail. And for a moment he once more considered shooting the hackamore rope that held his foot, only there was still no way he could get a clean sight on it without hitting the horse. The frightened animal, unable to buck because of the piece of timber, was crowhopping and trying to spin. He settled down at last and resumed his way down the bony trail, dragging the piece of wood and the man who was by now barely conscious.

Slocum had all but forgotten that he'd been shot in the shoulder, for his journey down the mountainside had taken on the quality of a scourging. He was beginning to wonder how long he might last.

After that last exchange with the man who had

tried to kill him he didn't remember much, only
that he was still on his back, his left leg pointing
skyward, and aware of the hard, uncomfortable ob-
ject under his right shoulder. It was the wood that
the horse had stepped through, so that it encircled
the pastern of the onside hind leg. He realized that
if it had been around any other hoof, the horse
would probably have kicked it off, but his own
weight prevented that, and so it served the double
purpose of a partial brake on the horse's movements
and a partial skid for the rider's battered, pendant
body.

It was the hackamore that had snared him—a
fifteen-foot length of manila coiled and tied on the
left side of the pommel. He was fortunate not to
have been caught in the stirrup, for the bronc probably would have kicked him to death. Being hung
at a higher angle, and farther forward, was one of
the two things that had saved him. The other was
the piece of wood.

He had been dragged through two creeks and
over brutal terrain. In vain he had tried to reach
one of the two pairs of long leather thongs used to
tie a slicker behind the cantle of the saddle. One
had come loose and was almost within reach, but
whenever he tried to push himself up by his left
hand to bring his right within reach, he pulled the
reins and the horse started plunging and attempting
to strike back at him with his onside forefoot. The
dangling stirrup was too far forward and too high.

There was one other possibility. If he could get
hold of the animal's tail, he had reasoned, he might
be able to pull himself up high enough so that his

left hand could seize either the stirrup or the loose tie string. But only a week earlier he had stopped at a ranch for a meal and had taken advantage of the pause in his journey to put the bronc in a squeeze gate, where he couldn't kick, and had carefully thinned and shortened the trailing tail—the sign of a wild range horse—and the tail was just a few inches out of reach.

He had just started riding the little bronc that spring, having spent most of the winter in the mountains, and so he had a snaffle bit with six-inch rings on his bridle, and the hackamore—a braided rawhide halter—in which his foot was snared, underneath. This was so he could picket the horse until such time as it learned to stand ground-hitched wherever the reins were dropped.

It had been early morning when he'd been shot, just at dawn, and the bushwhacker had followed him, shooting every now and again, Slocum returning the fire with his handgun. Had he hit him? Or had the killer run out of ammunition? Not likely. The man hadn't used up more than a dozen rounds. On the other hand, Slocum never had any notion that with his handgun he could hit his target. Only he'd had to do something—at the least, make his attacker cautious. He wondered again if he had hit him with a lucky shot. Or was the bushwhacker simply waiting for a better moment? Why hadn't he shot the horse? That would have immobilized Slocum completely, and he'd have been an easy target.

He began to be aware of coolness coming into the air and realized nightfall was not far off. Could he stay awake during the night? Was the other man waiting for dark, letting the long drag down the mountain do his work for him? Then he could simply slip up in the dark and either knife or club Slocum, who would be too exhausted to keep alert for very long.

But who was it? He didn't think it was any of the posse he had eluded at the beginning of winter. He knew them, knew they weren't the kind for bushwhacking, though they wouldn't hesitate to take what they called justice into their own hands. But this seemed more the work of a lone man. A bounty hunter? If so, who had hired him? It didn't matter who it was, really. He wished to God he had his skinning knife so that he could cut the hackamore rope, but it had been dragged off him along with his belt and most of his clothing as he'd been pulled along the trail.

Now the light was slanting across the valley, burning on the brown spots on his pony's hide. Later, a good while later—Slocum figured he must have passed out—the next thing he knew, the horse had stopped. When he opened his eyes he found himself looking into the barrel of a rifle.

"Stay right there," the very young voice said, "right where you are. And put your hands up."

"Holy shit!" mumbled the cut and bleeding man, and passed out.

# 2

Cold. On his cheeks, his back, his eyelids. He tried moving. Bound? He could move his fingers. And—pain. Gripping his shoulder like an iron ball. He thought of an Oregon boot, the great locked ball that kept prisoners from running away. His shoulder was an Oregon boot. And his chest; his chest was burning. And his back. All! All of him. A great throbbing white fire. And cool again. And the odor of . . . what? Something, something cool, fresh.

He opened his eyes and saw the girl bending over him. Her bosom was almost in his face, and he wanted to reach up, to reach out. But the light hurt his eyes and he closed them. He tried more carefully, looking through slitted eyelids.

He realized he was lying on his back in a bed. The bed was next to a log wall. He was in a log cabin. And he began to focus.

The girl, the woman, was bending over him. He smelled her. It was the freshness that had touched him at the beginning, that moment just before. Even the pain that gripped and twisted him couldn't stop that. Strangely, he felt safe, happy.

She was still bent over him, reaching for something next to the bed, then to his face which she touched with a soft, cool cloth. Now she touched along his neck and, gently drawing back the covers, began dabbing something onto his body. It was painful, but the feeling of being cared for outweighed the pain. She bent closer to him and a lock of her hair fell into his eyes. Even in his pain Slocum felt a stirring in him.

"Sorry." She straightened up, and then he saw her as she pushed wavy chestnut hair back from her clear, high forehead and smiled gently down at him.

He didn't speak, but lay there, drinking in her good looks. She had a soft, wide mouth and widely spaced eyes. Yet he knew it wasn't only that. It was . . . her. Her manner, her way, her . . . yes, her sound.

"Are you all right?" It was in her voice, too.

"What . . . Where am I?" His voice sounded strange to him and he closed his eyes again.

"You're much better," she said. "And where? You're in our house. Billy's and my house. I'm Sally. Sally Ellinger," she added quickly, and looked down, then back at him immediately. "The name doesn't mean anything to you. But we live here, my brother and I."

She reached down and pulled the covers back

over his body. "I'll do your legs now. Then you can do . . . the rest yourself."

"The rest?"

She looked at him, sternly puzzled, not sure how to take him as he suddenly placed himself as a man and not merely a patient lying helplessly dependent. Abruptly she turned toward his feet and lifted the covers. "Dr. Golightly says you must have this ointment on you. It will help stop any infection and you'll heal more quickly." She began applying the medicine to his legs.

Slocum still had a little trouble getting it straight, especially as her hand moved along his thigh with the cloth of ointment. He felt his erection rising and then felt her cover him again with the bed-clothes.

There was a slight flush on her face as she looked down at him and placed the cloth by his hand. "You had better do the rest. Do it now, while I'm getting you something to eat and drink. What would you like?"

Slocum was thinking that, pain or no pain, what he would like would be for the girl to come and lie beside him.

"I'd like you to take off your clothes and come lie down next to me," he said.

There was only a moment's pause till she said, "I don't believe you'd really like that; not with all those sores all over you, and the medicine. And besides, I don't want to do that."

He grinned, and it hurt, but it was all right. "I like you," he said.

"That's nice. Now, what would you like to eat?"

She was talking to him as though he was her kid brother, and he wanted to break out laughing, but even the suggestion of laughter hurt his body.

"Whatever you've got, miss."

"Sally."

"Sally."

"And your name?" She had walked to the door and now turned on the threshold.

"Slocum."

"Slocum what? Slocum Jones? Slocum Smith?"

"Just Slocum," he said.

She was dead serious. "I see. All right, Mr. Just Slocum. If you don't mind my being personal, I'll call you Just." She gave a little nod and then said, "You get that ointment on fast or you won't get any supper." And she was gone.

He lay there smiling to himself. Then he remembered the ointment and, pushing back the covers, he began to apply it. Fortunately, his crotch had escaped damage, but his buttocks and thighs were cut and bruised. Putting on the medicine tired him and he was glad when he was done. He had just pulled the covers over himself when she came back into the room.

"I've brought you some fresh water. Can you sit up to drink?"

"I don't think so."

She regarded him suspiciously. "You try. I'm cooking. It won't be long."

"Tell me what happened. I don't remember all of it. How I got here."

"Billy brought you in; or at least he came and got me and the two of us did it. But how you got here in the first place is another story. I don't know."

He closed his eyes as she went out, remembering the boy. Yes, the boy; he'd forgotten the boy. He couldn't have been more than twelve or thirteen. He remembered the rifle pointing at him and the kid telling him to throw up his hands. Likely it was that crazy demand that had made him pass out. If his life had depended on it at that instant he couldn't have moved a finger, let alone throw up his hands.

And when he had come to the boy was still there, still holding the Henry on him.

"God damn it!" he growled. "Don't stand there! Cut me free!"

The boy was short; he had on a huge Stetson hat with about the widest brim Slocum had ever seen. A mass of yellow hair spilled out from beneath it over his ears, into his eyes, past his shirt collar. He looked like a haystack. His clothes were too big, the trousers obviously hand-me-downs, which were supported by flaming red galluses. He was barefoot. Finally, there was a long blade of grass sticking out of his mouth; his face was of course heavily freckled. The word "hayseed" inevitably popped into Slocum's mind.

"Put yer gun down," the boy said, still gripping the Henry.

"Cut me free, for Christ's sake! Stop trying to be a goddamn sheriff or something!"

"You one of the Hamptons?"

"Hamptons? Shit, no. My name's Slocum. Now, God damn it . . . !" And Slocum dropped the Colt.

The boy lowered the rifle, albeit slowly, and now reached into a cavernous pocket of his enormous pants and drew forth a Barlow knife. He sniffed, wiped his nose with the back of his hand, and approached the man on the ground warily. Suddenly he thought of something and, pausing, kicked the handgun away, though it was already well out of Slocum's reach. The movement spooked the spotted bronc and Slocum was dragged a few yards before the horse settled down again.

"Jesus! You think you're some hot shit with that Henry, young feller! Put it down and cut me loose here!"

Now the boy stepped forward and cut the hackamore in one swift stroke. Slocum's leg dropped to the ground like a log and the pain shot through him like a wave of fire. He couldn't even curse before he lost consciousness.

"You still have fever," she said, and Slocum opened his eyes, feeling her cool palm on his forehead.

"Got any whiskey?"

"Yes, we do. Dr. Golightly said you'd likely ask, so he left some for you."

He watched her now as she took the bottle from the table near the bed. She was around twenty-five, he thought. She was not tall, but he could tell she had small bones, and while because he was lying down himself he couldn't really tell her height, he judged she'd probably come to his shoulder, being a six-footer himself. And once again, in spite of the pain in his feverish body, he thought of her lying beside him, and the fire hit his loins. He marveled at his desire; what a miracle, for he felt as though he'd been stomped by a dozen broncs, and yet his crotch ached in a quite different way from the rest of his body. It was good. It was good, and it helped him to handle the pain elsewhere.

The whiskey burned beautifully all the way through him. She was watching him.

"Go slowly," she said.

"I'm fine. Where's my horse?"

"He's in the corral. Billy has taken care of him."

"Billy's lucky he didn't get kicked. That little animal is a tough one."

She smiled, saying nothing, and he said, "You live alone here, the two of you?"

"Both our parents are dead." She looked away, then her eyes returned to him. "My father just . . . just not so long ago."

He didn't say anything. He waited.

"He was . . . well, he left us this place. A year ago." And she turned and left the room.

Slocum took another drink of the whiskey. Presently she was back with a tray of supper, and she helped him with his pillows so that he could raise up in order to eat.

"The doctor says you'll have to stay in bed a while and take it slowly for another good spell. You've had a rough time." Her eyes went to his shoulder. "Someone shot you."

"That's what I figured." And he managed a painful grin.

"I didn't think you'd shot yourself," she declared tartly. "But I won't do anything with that dressing now anyway. Dr. Golightly said to leave it. It's not too serious. It missed the bone."

She was standing close to the side of the bed,

and now she seemed to take an extra breath. "There's something I want to ask you."

"You want to know if I like you. Yes, I do—a lot."

"Stop funning. This is serious."

"You want to know if the law is after me."

"Yes, I do."

He liked the way she kept her eyes directly on him while they talked.

"Not any more. Not that I know about. There was a man, but I don't know who he was. He bushwhacked me. But that was a while back." He took a pull on the whiskey. "If you're worried, I'll saddle up and mosey along."

"You're not working with the Hamptons?"

"That's what Billy asked me."

"Better put down that whiskey and eat your soup and those biscuits. They're fresh. How long were you hung up with your horse like that?"

"I dunno. Longer than enough." He took the bowl of soup and the spoon from her. "You have nice eyes," he said. "What color are they?"

"Black." And she started out of the room.

Slocum finished the soup and two baking-powder biscuits, took another drink of whiskey, and lay back exhausted from the effort. There was a smile on his face as he thought of the girl. Her eyes were the bluest he had ever seen.

It had been a late spring, the snow staying long on the land. Each day was a unique brilliance, the high white peaks of the Rockies sparkling under the azure sky. It was not cold in the mountains, not during

the day; the air was dry, thin, tugging at the lungs
of a man not accustomed to that altitude. Below,
the melting snow and ice jammed the creeks,
overflowed the roaring Greybull as it rushed through
the long wide valley and on out to the south country.
High up on the rimrocks the ground was hard as
the iron on a wagon wheel, but down along the
banks of the river and in the meadows of the great
valley the land was soft and greening.

Each day Slocum remarked the weather. He was
mending, and the beauty of the land called him;
called his still tired body, his need for the nourish-
ment of nature, and a growing desire for action,
too. And so he chafed at having to rest, to spend
time in bed. At the same time he enjoyed the attention of the girl as she took care of him: cooking,
sewing his clothes, changing the dressing on his
wound, and getting the ointment on his back where
he couldn't reach. Once she paused at the scars of
two of his old wounds. He waited for her to say
something, but she didn't. Nor did she say anything
about the broad stripes a jailer's whip had made
across his back. He liked that.

He was glad he had spent the winter in the mountains, for the thin air had stretched his lungs so that
when he came down to a lower altitude he found,
as he always had, that he had extra energy. He
attributed much of his convalescence to this fact.
And to Sally Ellinger.

He had been at the cabin for a week now, and
the girl had become more relaxed with him, though
she was still somewhat on her guard. At first he
had thought her reserve was because of fear that he

might be connected with the Hamptons, whoever they were. He realized he had ridden into, or rather been dragged into, some sort of feud, but he hadn't asked her any pointed questions. He felt no need to question. He didn't really care; he simply wanted to get well.

As the time passed he found his thoughts turning more and more to the girl, and he began to watch her more closely, admiring the soft yet sure way she moved, the way she did things, the way she handled her young brother. At the same time, Slocum felt her opening toward him, reaching out, and then closing. He didn't push her. He didn't mind her ambivalence; he had himself. He was a man on his own terms who could take things as they came.

The doctor came. Anse Golightly: tall, stringy, with a hoarse voice, bright bronze eyes, and a lot of extra flesh on his face and body. Except for his hands. These were meticulously formed and, when he was working with a patient, knew exactly what they were doing. His touch was gentle, sure, and quick. His tongue, on the other hand, was sharp, sure, and quick.

"If you don't take care of that shoulder, Slocum, I'd say you got less sense than whoever it was thought he could kill you."

Slocum had noticed something in Golightly's manner. The doctor glanced every now and again toward the window, as though anticipating something, as though his attention had been listening for some sound. Was he expecting something? Sally Ellinger had explained prior to Golightly's arrival that it might be difficult to get him to come out to the ranch, but she hadn't said why.

"I'll do like you say, Doc," Slocum said, grinning at the long man standing beside the bed. "I am not in any position where I could do different, I'd say."

Doc Golightly allowed a smile to glance off those bronze eyes as he looked down at his patient. Slocum had the sudden feeling that he wanted to stay there, but at the same time was feeling pressed to go.

"How about some coffee, Dr. Golightly?" Sally asked brightly as she came into the room.

"Got to be going," Doc said. His careful white hands were already returning things to the black bag.

"But it's still light," Sally insisted. "Do you have another patient out this way?"

Something in the exchange caught Slocum. There was more than just the words there.

"It'll be dark soon enough," Doc said, his voice gruff with impatience. Then he caught himself. Looking down at the man in the bed, he said, "You mind what Sally here tells you." His tone was genial for the first time since his arrival. His eyes went to the girl. "You could bring him into town next time. About a week. You've got a gig, have you? He shouldn't ride for a spell."

She didn't answer, seeming to accept that she would be driving Slocum into town in a week's time.

"You worried about the law, Doc?" Slocum asked suddenly as Golightly picked up the black bag and straightened up tall. "It wasn't the law shot me."

"The law?" Golightly let the bag rest on the foot

of the bed. His big eyes went from Slocum to the girl and back to Slocum. "The law?" he repeated. "I tell you, I wish there *was* law in this valley. No, I am not worried about the law. I am worried about the lack of it."

He picked up the bag and, with a nod at his patient, started out of the room. "Sally, a word with you." And he put his long arm around the girl's shoulders for an instant, dropping it as she preceded him out the door.

He could hear them talking outside the room, but their words were indistinct, and he had no wish to overhear them anyway. Then there was silence, and he heard Golightly riding off at a brisk canter.

He sat up and carefully moved his legs out of the covers so that his feet were on the floor. He waited, testing his strength, then stood. It wasn't the first time. He had been practicing, had even walked to the window a few times, but the girl didn't know it.

"I might have known." She scolded him gently as she came into the room, as she would a child caught in some naughtiness. "Now you get right back into bed. You've no business being up. You could even start your bleeding again."

He had turned to face her. "What's eating Golightly?"

"He thinks somebody might be watching the ranch," she said. "I don't know if he's being overly suspicious, or maybe it's true. Now please get back into bed."

"What do you really think?"

"It could be true."

He was standing close to her and now he put his hands on her shoulders, looking down into her face.

"I'll be pulling out," he said, "directly it's dark."

She was looking right into his eyes, her mouth slightly open in surprise. He was aware of the heat of her body and he thought he couldn't stand it another minute. But he took hold of himself; this was not the time for what he had in mind, much as he wished it.

"No," she said.

"If there's somebody out there, it could be for me, and I don't want you and Billy involved. It's my business."

"No," she said again, and took a step away from him, while keeping her eyes right on his face.

He dropped his arms. There was something extra in her voice that he just barely caught.

She was standing very still with her hands together at her waist, looking at him earnestly. And then she said, "Slocum, I'm not so sure that whoever is out there watching the cabin is after you."

He had waited for the full dark, figuring to track the man by sound rather than sight. Slocum had always believed in a brisk offense and surprise. If it was the bounty hunter out there he would likely be settled down for a long watch and not expect his quarry to start hunting him.

And listening would be a better means than seeing for Slocum in his weakened condition. It was a gamble, for he still wasn't all that sure of his muscles, his reflexes. Yet to remain in the cabin under the circumstances, knowing that somebody was out there—either someone waiting for him, or for the two Ellingers—needed to be settled.

She had argued with him not to go, pointing out all the obvious things. He was still weak, he'd have trouble in any kind of encounter, especially hand-to-hand. And also, because of his weakened condition he would likely not be as quiet as he would need to be.

"What makes you think it's somebody out there for you?" he had asked her.

"I'm an Ellinger. I guess you haven't heard of the Hampton–Ellinger feud. Billy and I and our parents were related to Cole Ellinger and all his brothers and sisters and sons and daughters; the whole clan."

"And so you're on the Hampton target list."

"We've more or less managed to keep out of it. Dad only moved here a little while ago, not knowing what was going on, but wanting to be near family. We're originally from Ohio. But..." And she had looked down at her hands. "We didn't know the Hamptons and Ellingers were going to start trying to kill each other off. That's... that's how our dad died. A stray bullet."

"It's still a bullet, isn't it," he said softly. And then he added, "Why?"

"Cattle. I'm not sure I know all of it. But please get back into bed." She stood looking at him a little defiantly, as though challenging him to challenge her. "There have been two men shot already, besides Dad. I grieve. I grieve for Dad, but killing the Hamptons isn't going to bring him back to life." And then: "Into bed!"

In the end he had seen that she would continue to argue with him and he didn't want to wear himself out, so he simply agreed, saying he was tired, and he turned in.

He lay in his bed waiting, until he figured she had to have fallen asleep. More than an hour passed before he got up and dressed, buckled on the Colt, and slipped out of the cabin. He knew she was up, even though there was no light coming from beneath the door of her room; he could feel something in the house. It was not a house that was sleeping. He paused for a moment near the alcove where Billy was lying in his bedroll on the floor.

The moon was down and in the pitch dark Slocum moved slowly toward the barn, testing himself for strength and agility, accepting the pain as his skin, called to movement now, tore him. Moving slowly, he listened with every part of his body, not just with his ears. The old Indian who had taught him so many things about tracking had taught him just that—to listen beyond the sounds, to the vibrations. To listen with his skin. It was how he'd known she was up and not sleeping—listening with his torn, stinging skin.

Softly he slipped past the barn down the short draw on the far side and, bent low, moved up toward the fringe of timber that would have been the logical place for a man to hide out while watching the Ellinger cabin. For he knew that if it was the man who had tried to kill him, he would pick the logical place. He knew this from the way the man had followed him when his horse was dragging him down the mountain, the way he had shot at him.

He also knew he was right-handed and probably over six feet tall. A careful man, he put it to himself, logical and not very intuitive, if at all. A stranger to the mountains. For when a man tracks you trying to kill you, you get to know him. You get to know him in a way you never would otherwise.

The moon had risen; it stood in the sky off to his right as he entered the cottonwoods. Now he waited just inside the rim of trees, listening to the rhythm of the nearby creek, the softly popping land with its ceaseless night sounds and movement. He moved further into the trees, swallowed by the smell of bark and leaves, the night breath filling him with the richness he knew so well. Suddenly the weakness swept him, and his head spun. His whole body felt raw and without any force.

He was only a little way inside the trees, yet he could see nothing. Dark as a gun barrel was the thought that came to his mind. He wanted to sit down, to rest, but he forced himself to remain standing, taking a strong grip on himself, as he waited close to a clump of bullberry bushes.

He could hear nothing other than the ordinary night sounds. After an hour had passed he was about to decide that Golightly must have made a mistake when suddenly the wind stirred through the thick trees and he smelled the horse. At once every fiber in his body was keened. Now he heard the soft jingle of a bridle, the squeak of leather. Yet in the dark pit of the trees he could still see nothing.

Carefully he moved back to the edge of the cottonwoods, where the moonlight had just broken through. He stood just inside the trees, looking

down at the Ellinger cabin. He had moved with
every caution, hoping that any noise he might make
due to his physical weakness would be covered by
the movement of the man and the horse. Indeed,
the man and his horse were making noise openly
now, as though the man had no fear that would
make him try to conceal his presence.

The sky was not wholly clear, Slocum saw. There
were large, scudding clouds, and the wind was
stronger. Once again the moon was hidden, this
time behind a bank of clouds. And now again the
clouds had moved and the whole land was bathed
in the silver light of the moon.

Yet the man, for all the noise he was making,
had enough savvy not to step immediately out of
the line of trees, but waited until another large cloud
darkened the land.

Slocum waited. And when the man stepped out
leading his horse, Slocum moved away from the
tree which had concealed him.

"Hold it right there!"

Slocum had taken the risk, fearing that if he
waited till it was more clear, the man would get
away.

The man was just ahead of the horse, leading
him, but at the instant of Slocum's ringing challenge, he ducked, darting to the far side of the
horse, just as Slocum—not as fast as he could have
been—fired.

The horse's scream rent the night air, and the
man, who evidently had not been hit, turned and
raced away down the hill just as an even thicker
body of cloud completely covered the moon. Slocum

fired again where he thought the fleeing figure was headed. It was a useless gesture. Meanwhile, the horse had bolted.

There was no sense in attempting to follow. Slocum, again extremely weak, began to walk down the hill toward the cabin. It was a long walk, but soon he heard the girl calling him. He called back that he was all right.

"Oh, God!" she cried, running toward him, followed by Billy. "I didn't know what had happened. I knew you went out. And I waited. I heard the shooting and the horse. Are you all right?"

"I'm all right. He must have been watching the house. But who he was I've no notion." He smiled down at her upturned face as they started to walk together toward the cabin.

"Did you hit him?" the boy asked. "Maybe he's badly wounded. He could bleed to death!"

"Billy!"

"Well, what was he doing spying on us then!" He bit out the words defensively as he walked in long strides next to Slocum, answering his sister, who was on the other side of the big man.

"I'll go up when it's daylight and see what I can read of his sign," Slocum said.

"I'll help," Billy offered assertively.

"Billy!" His sister's voice was sharp.

"We'll see," Slocum said, and his two companions subsided.

Together they escorted him to the cabin, got him into bed, and brought hot soup.

"Was it one of the Hamptons?" Billy was chewing vigorously on the grass stem which seemed never to leave him. "Was it?" Though still sleepy, he was bristling with questions and excitement, ignoring his sister, who told him again to get back to bed.

When finally the boy left them the girl brought a glass of whiskey.

"Drink this and get right to sleep,"she said. "You've probably set yourself back another week or two."

"Maybe. Maybe not."

"You're so pigheaded," she said.

"Maybe I better pull out. Don't want to overstay it here."

"Stop that now. This is no time for teasing. You get right to sleep. I've got Billy's rifle here in case anyone takes a notion to come by."

"You know how to shoot it?" He grinned up at her.

"Don't be a smart aleck," she snapped, but he could tell she liked the teasing. "Do you think it was someone after you?" she asked. "Or one of the Hamptons?"

"Don't know. Like I said, I'll know more in the morning."

"You're going to stay right here in the morning."

"Will you stay with me?"

"I will be seeing to it that you don't leave the house. Tomorrow you're going to stay in bed."

"There's only one way you can keep me in bed, miss."

"That's enough of that."

"No, it's not enough," Slocum said. "We haven't even begun to get started, let alone even think of it as being anywhere near enough!"

And she had to grin at him as he lay back, satisfied with having scored his point, a big smile on his face.

Then, despite all that he wanted, despite his desire, his eyes closed and he fell fast asleep.

The girl stood looking down at him. "Sleep well," she said. And her eyes gazed over his strong yet tired face.

The next morning, overriding her protests, and supported in his decision by Billy, Slocum walked up to take a look at the area where the man had been watching the ranch. The boy came with him; Sally stayed at home with her chores. It was washday, and she had let him set up the pole for her washing.

It was a clear day with the sun warm and shining on his back and shoulders as he and Billy walked carefully up to where he had shot at the man the night before.

"A big horse," Slocum said, studying the hoofprints. "About to go lame in his off hind foot. Indicates the rider either doesn't know horses or doesn't give a damn. Likely both. So he's no cowhand, and likely earns his living with his gun."

He took a long time combing over the area where the man had waited the night before, finding a rag with oil on it, and some blood. "He takes care of his guns but not his animals," Slocum said, muttering the words as he squatted, studying the sign carefully. The boy, chewing as always, watched him with intense eyes.

He stood up from his squatting position, stretching carefully. "He was wearing trail boots. He's over six feet, chews tobacco pretty steady, I'd say, and he had whiskey with him."

"Golly!" said the boy, and his blue eyes goggled while he whipped off his big hat, his yellow hair spilling all over the place, then slammed the hat down on his head again.

"We gonna track him, are we?" He was bursting with excitement. Slocum could almost see his heart pounding.

"He's long gone. Wouldn't settle much to follow him. We could, but I ain't in all that good shape." He said it half jesting, and the boy took it up.

"I'll be with you. I'm feeling great!"

Slocum grinned. "He'll turn up again," he said. "And we'll see if you're still feeling great."

"No worry about that, by golly." His grin looked as though it would spread to his ears, if it could find them under all that hair. "How long's he been here?" the boy asked when he had calmed down a little.

"Couple of days."

"Can you tell why?"

Slocum regarded the boy carefully. "You sure ask a lot of questions. Why do you think he was here? Looking for a lost gold mine or something, for Christ's sake?"

He watched the boy's cheeks redden, but those blue eyes didn't drop. They still looked up at the tall man, grinning like a happy lynx who had just swallowed a bird.

"He must've been scouting us."

When they were back in the cabin he told the

girl, "If it's someone looking for me he'll turn up, and if it's someone watching you he'll turn up. My notion is he's the one who shot me. Those prints show he's moving slow. I doubt if he's a Hampton he'd be out there wounded, like I figure he is. They'd have sent someone more in one piece. And besides, why would they want to watch your house? You're for sure no threat to them, are you?"

"Cole, my uncle, says that our ranch is right in the way of a trail drive they're planning. They'll be moving the cattle up onto the mountain. Cole says we're right in the way, being in the center of this narrow part of the valley. With me and Billy here they'd have to go around by Ten Fork."

"The Hamptons."

She nodded. "They were willing to go around before, before the fighting, and when their herd was smaller. But now they won't want to take that time and trouble. They've got a lot of cattle now."

"But you've had nothing to do with the fighting."

"It doesn't matter. We're Ellingers, Billy and I."

His eyes went to the open window, catching the flight of a meadowlark as it sang through the framed sky.

"You must be lonely," he said suddenly, turning back to her.

She looked away from him for a moment and then she said, "Not really. I have my life. I have Billy, and the ranch. I have my life," she repeated, and there was not a grain of sorrow in her voice.

Later, when the boy was out doing chores, she began her narration slowly, telling him about the

Hamptons and the Ellingers and their feud in Sunshine Basin.

"I don't know how it ever got started. Dad told me some of it, Cole too, and, well . . . everyone." A laugh started in her throat. "To be near the family, Dad told us. And that's what Mother wanted, too. But she died less than a year after we got here. That's ten years ago, when we came. Everybody in the Ellinger and Hampton families were friendly then. Even Old Hamp."

"Did the other Ellingers, your cousins, come out here long before you?"

"I don't know, exactly. Maybe three, four years. Anyway, it was about the same time as the Hamptons. Both families moved into the Basin and built homes about ten miles apart."

"Just by chance?"

"Like I said, they were good friends in those days. They wanted to be close. Then it seems they began working for Barney Ziegler; some of them. Barney owns the Lazy Z up north of the basin. He's the biggest outfit in this part of the country. The way Dad told it, both families worked on and off for Barney and some other outfits, though mostly Barney, and meanwhile began building up herds of their own."

Slocum caught the rueful note in her words. "I see—in the usual way cowhands often build herds for themselves."

"Dad said they rustled."

"That's what I'm saying. A little bit here, a head or two there. Branding the slicks, and who knows the difference. It happens all over."

"I didn't realize that, I guess."

"Most of the big ranchers tolerate a little here and there. It's real hard to stop. But you're saying it got out of hand."

"That's how Dad put it. For a while the families were sort of working together, or at least letting the other do whatever they wanted, but then something went wrong."

"They got greedy; that's what went wrong."

"Yes. That's it."

"What about Barney Ziegler? Were they still working for him?"

"Yes, they were. He got wind of it and they were kicked out. Of course, by then they had herds of their own and didn't need him."

"But they needed the grass and water."

"Dad said Hamp Hampton tried to get the Ellingers to join them and fight Barney Ziegler and the other ranchers in the Basin. But Cole, Uncle Cole wouldn't go along."

"I take it Cole is sort of head of the Ellinger clan."

She nodded. And then she said, "But it isn't all that easy, that simple and clear."

He watched the sunlight playing on her chestnut hair as she sat by the window. She was looking down at her hands, which were lying in her lap. He waited, seeing she had more to tell.

"It's not that simple. Because the families ... well, there were certain relationships between some of the members."

"I'm sure of that. What can you expect, living

within ten miles of each other way out here in nowhere."

"Some got married. And some didn't." Suddenly she stood up and, turning so that her back was to him, she faced the window. "I don't know why I'm telling you. Maybe I just can't not tell someone."

When he saw her drop her head and the movement of her shoulders he rose and walked to where she was standing, crying softly into whatever it was that had happened to her.

"I'm sorry." She straightened, dabbed at her eyes, and started out of the room. "I'm sorry. I shouldn't have let it go so far."

"Why don't you tell me the whole thing?" he said. "Get it out. It could help."

She stood in the doorway facing him. "Thank you. Thank you for listening. Maybe another time."

It was the day he first tried getting on a horse again. But he didn't try the spotted bronc. He picked a blaze-faced bay gelding that seemed pretty tough, sparky enough for his purpose.

It felt good being in the saddle again. He had felt the pain in his shoulder as he'd swung up and over, but he was in pretty good shape now.

"You sure you can handle that, Slocum?" Sally said, looking at him from the corral gate.

"I am fine," he answered, "for an old codger."

He liked the way she laughed. He looked over at Billy, who was riding a neat little strawberry roan. They were heading into town for a few things, and on the way they would check over some of the Double E beeves; a small herd of about a hundred

head left them by their father Harry Ellinger, and
cared for now by Sally and Billy and, when needed,
some of their uncle Cole's men.

It was again a day newly minted with the sunlight
dancing on the wings of the meadowlarks, on the
stems of the grass that carpeted the meadow, and
he felt it warm on his hands, on his shoulders, on
his thighs as he rode silently alongside Billy.
Rounding a low cutbank, they suddenly came upon
a small herd of mule deer. They had all come to a
stop, the two horsemen and the feeding deer, to
look at each other in wonder. It was a good moment.
Then, without any apparent signal, yet they all knew
the precise moment, the deer bounded away, their
white tails bobbing out of sight as they entered the
treeline at the edge of the meadow.

Slocum watched the boy's profile as they rode.
He was sitting easy in an old stock saddle, chewing
the long stem of grass that hung from his mouth.
He looked like his sister, though the lines of his
face were definitely male. Yet he had that same
humor in his eyes, and a way of ducking his head
slightly when he talked, just like her.

"I'll be pulling out directly," Slocum said.

The boy turned, his jaw dropping, but the stem
of grass didn't fall. "Why? What for?"

"Got things to do."

"Sis and I wuz saying so just last night. Figgered
you'd be riding on."

Slocum took a quirly out of the pocket of his
hickory shirt and lighted it with a lucifer.

"Wisht you'd change your mind," the boy said.

And he added, "We could use another hand around the ranch."

"We'll run into each other again," Slocum said. "Meanwhile, I'll buy you a sarsaparilla in town."

"Haw! And you'll be drinking beer!"

"Whiskey," Slocum said.

# 3

Some old-timers put it that the town had been thrown together in the week God took to make the rest of the world; others said it had been left by a tornado. It was in the middle of no place at all, like something that had just fallen onto the prairie and was maybe waiting to be blown away. No one knew why there was a town right there. There were ranches, to be sure: Barney Ziegler's big Lazy Z, and the Ellingers' and the Hamptons', and half a dozen others. But for the needs of those folk, nearby Tensleep would have served better. It had better saloons, better gambling facilities, and better girls. But for some mysterious reason Sunshine Basin— known really as "The Town"—had something that Tensleep apparently lacked. Possibly it was the simple fact that Tensleep tried to be a town, even had

a marshal and the beginnings of a school, while
The Town, which had started as Robber's Roost, a
sort of spa for outlaws who wished to retire from
public notice for a while, just didn't give a damn.
For sure, it was a go-to-hell place with the hair on,
and most of the doors swung both ways. But indeed
there was a marshal, and he was permanent; six
feet under in the middle of Main Street this good
while.

Slocum and the boy rode slowly down Main
Street, their horses stirring up little plumes of dust.
They rode in silence, Slocum taking in the store-
fronts: McHone's General Store, the Okay Eatery,
the Denver House, the barber—bath—undertaker, the
four saloons, and Sister Ellie's cathouse. Sister
Ellie's was the first establishment anyone came to
riding in from the North Fork, and so it was with
Slocum and Billy Ellinger. Billy pointed it out to
Slocum, and Slocum noted that as the boy spoke
his slow chewing of the stalk of grass increased in
speed with, Slocum thought, a certain agitation.
Indeed, he felt it himself, thinking that he might at
some point sample the wares in Sister's establishment. But such thoughts turned his attention toward
Sally Ellinger, and her cool evasion of what was
beginning to interest him more and more.

He rode with care, without moving his head
much. Like any man seasoned to the trail or to town
dangers, he knew you could see a lot more if you
didn't stare directly, if you didn't get taken by what
you were looking at. At the same time, he realized
that someone was watching them from the big
downstairs window of the unpainted building, which

had many of its clapboards curled and sprung from the frame. Sister Ellie's resembled a big blister, curled by the sun and stripped of its covering. Clearly, no fancy frills.

Yes, there was definitely someone watching. Of course, it could be somebody sizing up the weather. And now he turned his head and looked directly at the woman standing in the window. He couldn't make out her features, but he felt her youth and, when she waved, her availability. He grinned back at her, not sure she could see his expression, which was partly hidden by the wide brim of his hat. He felt better. He felt a lot better.

The hitchracks were crowded, so they decided on the livery stable, but then Slocum spotted a place just outside the Hard Winter Saloon, which stood between McHone's General Store and the Frontier Gaming Room.

Dismounting, Slocum felt the twinge in his shoulder and back, but he was glad to find that in general the ride hadn't hurt him. Stepping up onto the wooden sidewalk, he saw the shingle hanging over the small doorway next to the general store. The lettering revealed that this was the office of Dr. Anson Golightly, and the hours were listed. But the sign was in need of paint, and Slocum had to squint to read all of it.

In the general store a heavy-set man in yellow galluses and a beard greeted them.

"I am needing some ammo," Slocum said, approaching the worn wooden counter and eyeing the packed shelves that ran from wall to ceilling.

The storekeeper's eyes flicked to the holstered

Colt at his customer's hip. Then his glance moved
to Billy. "Some jawbreaker, Billy?"

"Sure," the boy said, and grinned.

"Two boxes will do me for now," Slocum said.
"And that Barlow knife there."

"First time in this country?" the storekeeper
asked. He was a large man with a long nose, the
tip of which was red. He flushed some as his customer accepted the ammunition without answering
his question.

"Quiet in town," he resumed. "My name is Cal
McHone. I've known Billy there since he was a
button." He chuckled. "I reckon he still is, for the
matter of that."

"He can handle himself," Slocum said. And he
could feel McHone backwashing as he blinked and
colored slightly, as though he'd stuck his foot in it.
Slocum had spoken low on purpose so the boy
wouldn't hear him.

McHone was about to say something to that when
Slocum saw his eyes dart to the door of the shop,
which was directly behind him, and Slocum heard
the door open.

"Good morning, Mr. McHone." The voice was
musical, and with it came a whiff of a subtle perfume and the rustle of skirts.

The proprietor of McHone's General Store was
beaming and perspiring at the same time. John
Slocum made a point of not turning right away, but
instead remained with his eyes on McHone, as
though nothing had happened.

"How much do I owe you?" Slocum said, staring
right at McHone.

The storekeeper, tearing his eyes away from the woman who had entered his establishment, mumbled the price.

Only when he had paid did Slocum pick up his purchases and turn. In so doing he noticed that young Billy Ellinger was staring with his mouth open; he'd even forgotten to chew on his blade of grass.

And in the next instant Slocum saw why. She was average height, with a figure fitting perfectly the description used by writers of novels—hourglass; her beauty was matched only by her radiance and charm. Brown eyes, black hair hanging to her shoulders, covering the top of her white silk blouse, which housed a firm but obviously resilient bosom, the nipples of which were not totally concealed. It flashed through Slocum that possibly those nipples had hardened in response to himself. He trusted that it might be so, for he had himself hardened, so that his trousers felt they were going to rip.

"I am Felicia Ziegler," she said. "You appear to be a stranger in town."

"I'm Slocum, miss. John Slocum."

Her brown eyes danced along his face, focusing for an instant on his lips.

On the other side of the counter, McHone gave a start as he heard the name. And Slocum caught his reaction in the mirror that was hanging near him on the wall.

Felicia Ziegler was obviously in her early twenties. Taking a step toward him, she held out her hand. "Welcome to Sunshine Basin, Mr. Slocum." And, washing his face slowly with her dazzling smile, she turned to McHone. "Is the fabric I ordered in from Denver?"

As they left the store, Slocum saw that Billy was grinning.

"You got something on your mind, young feller?"

"Yup. I bet you have, too, by golly."

Slocum stared at him, stopping in his tracks at the edge of the boardwalk. "How old are you?"

"Old enough."

"Boy, I sure guess you are!" Slocum broke into a roar of laughter.

The Sunshine Basin visit was starting to have its bright moments, he decided, as he told Billy to find something for himself to do for a bit while he went on up to visit Doc Golightly.

It was Doc who fleshed out the history and gossip of the Sunshine Basin War. Slocum had come to have his arm and shoulder checked, but he had also come for information. A town doctor, like a barber, knows everything that's going on. In his home territory, Doc was in good form. Sock-footed, he clomped around the tiny office on his huge feet, pouring milk for his cat, Thaddeus.

His examination was quick and sure. He ended with a slight tap on the mended shoulder, like it was a blackboard and he was giving a lecture. "Sound. Sound as a dollar; you can bet on it. Be stiff for a spell, but I know you'll take care of limbering it up." He paused, sniffing. Then, bending, he inspected his patient's back, ribs, and legs— his whole body in fact.

"Sound!" Another sniff. "You are in your prime. Lucky. That drag down the mountain would've killed

an older man or a younger one." He cocked his
head, studying the man seated beneath his examining hands. "You'll need to be in good condition
if you're aiming to stick around The Town here, or
the Basin. I got a notion that you are intending just
that—not that I butt into anyone's private business.
But, you being a patient of mine, I just thought I'd
pass on the caution."

"How are you meaning that?" Slocum asked.

"I am saying that if you have any sense you'll
just mosey on. You're already marked, you know.
Stayin' out there with Sally Ellinger."

"And Billy."

"The folks only see it as Sally. And you know
what I mean." He held up the palm of his long hand
to stem any objection from his patient as he swept
on, the words coming out wet as he sprayed saliva
gently about the room. "I just don't mean the pleasures of the flesh, young feller. I am talking guns.
People have heard of you, Slocum. I have heard of
John Slocum. They say you rode with Quantrill,
amongst other items. Like—fast with a gun. Tough
as whang leather. Friendly up to a point which it
don't take too long to reach. And you like to travel
light—meaning, without taking prisoners. You get
the picture?"

"I do."

"Is it accurate?"

"I wouldn't dream of doubting you, Doc. You
have got me down to a T."

"On the other hand," Doc swept along, "or foot,
if you've a notion, she's done a damn good job
with that outfit out there by the North Fork, and

raising that boy and all. Make a man a nice wife, I'd say. By God, if I had ten years off I'd be dancing attendance on that gal. She is pretty, too. Real good-looking, not fleshy like that little Ziegler thing. . . ."

"Felicia Ziegler?"

Doc took a step back and surveyed his patient, his mouth forming a big O. "By jingo, you have cottoned onto her already." His eyes closed, his cheeks reddened, and his jowels began to quiver. Slocum realized he was laughing.

"By God, how do you like that! You do not waste a minute, do you, by God! I like that! I by-God like that!" And he slapped Slocum on his wounded shoulder so that he winced.

"Sorry!" He was all apology on the instant, concern wiping all the fun off his face. "Sorry, just got carried away." He stepped quickly across the room. "We'll have a little refreshment here. I know you've got the time. I know you want to hear what's been going on around here."

Fascinated, Slocum watched him locate a bottle, after a certain amount of searching, and two glasses which he placed on his examining table and into which he poured liberally.

"Your health." Doc held his glass high.

"And yours." Slocum followed suit, glad for the drink.

"Now I'm going to fill you in on the doings. You want to hear? Well, I'm going to tell you," he went on, not waiting for an answer. "First blood, if I could put it that way, first blood of the Sunshine Basin War leaked out of Barney Ziegler's range foreman, Johnny Gilhooly. Remember, the Ellingers and the Hamptoms had been stealing Ziegler's stock to a fare-thee-well, and were at the point of fighting each other over who was getting what. The boys were touchy all round, is what I'm saying." Pausing a moment for refreshment, Doc plunged on. "One day in the fall of the year Johnny buckled on his gun—I treated him following the passage at arms that ensued, and so I got it first hand—and rode south on a mission that was growing old for him. Not too much time passes before he encounters Miles Hampton." Doc paused. "Miles being one of Old Hamp Hampton's feisty sons." He had been moving back and forth as he spoke, telling his story with gestures and body movements, and now he swept into dialogue, as though he was acting out a play.

"'I'm looking for a bunch of Ziegler's horses that somebody rustled last night,' Johnny said. I can imagine, and so can you likely imagine, Miles's dark face—some say he has Injun or Mex in him—getting darker at those pregnant words. 'Well,' says Miles, 'What the hell are you looking for 'em on Hampton range for?'

"'By God, I can't think of a more likely place to look,' Johnny comes back at him. You can see, Slocum, this is what those Eastern scriveners call 'blunt fighting talk.' And both of those raunchy boys went for their weapons. When the smoke cleared, Johnny was riding home with a hole in his leg, and Miles was heading for the Hampton spread with rage in his heart. Result? The Hamptons were— all of 'em, right down to the youngest—furious at having their sweet virtue questioned, and they all of 'em swore to get even with Barney Ziegler and any other ranchers in the vicinity who might take a notion to side with him."

"Like the Ellingers."

"Like the Ellingers, and anybody else, too. But especially the Ellingers, on account of Hamp Hampton thinking Cole and his bunch were cheating them on the slicks they were all stealing, and especially on account of what happened with our friend." He paused, while Slocum lifted his eyebrows.

"I see you're interested," Doc swept on. "Well, you should be. And I shouldn't be telling you this. So—you have Burt Hampton, another son, walking out with Sally Ellinger; you get the picture. They was closer than two gnats inside a barrel of honey. Folks were hearing wedding bells. But..."

"But he threw her over, or she threw him over." Slocum hadn't particularly wanted to speak, but it was necessary to stem the tide of words flowing from Doc, not to mention the tidal spray of saliva which accompanied his narrative.

"Wrong! You are wrong!" Doc wiped his mouth with the back of his wrist, then paused swiftly to down a good dollop of whiskey. "Something happened." He stopped dramatically, those big bronze eyes shining, the way a teacher will look at his favorite pupil as he coaxes his understanding of a knotty problem.

"He got her..."

"...in a family way." Doc couldn't wait; the words broke from him in triumph. "Burt Hampton got Sally Ellinger with child, and it was soon evident. Then . . . ?" He paused again, eyeing his "pupil."

"Then he refused to marry her."

"Go to the head of the class!"

Slocum was glad he'd sent Billy off on his own; otherwise, he'd never have heard this part of the jigsaw puzzle. Yet he had suspected something extra . . . something that was more than just a matter of cows.

"And the child?"

Doc's voice was dead sober as he said, "The child did not live."

"And Burt Hampton?"

"Burt left the country; with Cole Ellinger—after Sally's father died—swearing vengeance. Burt has not been heard of since. Uh . . . until recently."

"He's back?"

"I dunno." Doc squinted at Thaddeus, who had finished the milk and was stretching in the beam of sunlight that was slanting through the dirty window glass. "I dunno. There is talk that Burt was seen down around Rockland."

"It could be he's coming back, and that will add to the excitement."

"You got the picture." Doc beamed, sighed, moved to a splattered spittoon, and ejected a mouthful of saliva. "Shit take it. This town has never had it without some goddamn thing pulling at it. Just when everyone thought we wuz going to settle down to a nice, steady range war, we get news of Burt Hampton making tracks for home, and you can bet your bottom dollar he will not be without a lot of armaments about his person."

"What kind is he?" Slocum asked.

"Not the kind you'd want to meet. Can't figger what she ever saw in such a one. But women are strange. You ever notice that, Slocum? I'll bet you have," he added without waiting.

Slocum nodded. "Women are strange, that's for sure," he said. "And so are men. *Humans* are strange."

Doc was eyeing him. "You say that like you mean it."

"I do. I like 'em, for the most part. Humans. But they ain't natural."

A deep chuckle came rolling out of Golightly's long throat. "I know what you mean. A horse . . . hell, he's a horse, and a cow's a cow. But a human. Shit, I dunno what the hell a human is."

"But I like them," Slocum insisted. "Some of them."

"Especially the ones that wear skirts," Doc said, and he lifted his glass appreciatively. "Here's to the fair sex. God bless 'em."

Then Doc fell strangely silent. Finally he said, "I delivered Sally's baby. Some of the women wanted to run her out of the country. And of course the Hamptons wanted to, and even some of the Ellingers. But the Hamptons—now get this!—figuring she'd done the dirty on Burt!"

"But not Cole."

"Cole backed her. Cole . . . Cole is a man; her father's brother, and when Harry Ellinger got hit by that stray bullet—I tended him, too—Cole stood by Sally, and when she had her trouble, too. He's a good man." Then he said, "Shit." And when

Slocum cut his eye at him fast to see what was wrong, he said, "Forgot. Cole's been owing me five dollars this good while."

They parted shortly after, but not without Golightly warning him to be careful, especially if Burt Hampton came home to the Basin and discovered Slocum living out at the Double E ranch.

"But they broke apart a long while back, you tell me."

"That's right. Except Burt, he's always been a possessive, jealous bugger. He's not apt to take kindly to what he once considered his property and could be still considers—living under the same roof with a man named John Slocum."

"That's not my concern," Slocum snapped, getting to his feet.

Doc grinned, and dealt his second ace. "Then maybe this is. The news is that the Hamptons hired a special gunman . . . sent all the way to Fort Worth for him."

"So?"

"I don't reckon that is yourself, but there could be some around these parts who do figure you are him." He took a final swallow from his glass. "Or, if they don't figure you're really that gunslinger from Texas, they'll figure you for another gun, sent for by the Ellingers. Either way, Slocum. You can't beat it. You're in the middle in more ways than one. And I'd say you better watch it. I am only warning you." He held up his long hand. "Only warning you. And I am telling you you'd be smart to saddle up and ride."

He found Billy waiting downstairs on the board-

walk working on a fresh stick of jawbreaker candy.
Now, following his talk with Anse Golightly, Slocum
found himself looking at the boy in a different way,
as though they were closer than they had been.

As they rode down the street with the late afternoon sun slanting into the riffling dust stirred by
their horses, he suddenly looked over at the Denver
House. Felicia Ziegler had just come out and was
standing on the boardwalk with her hand on her hip
looking up and down the street as though undecided
which way to go. Riding past her, Slocum caught
her eyes on him, and touched the brim of his hat.
Her smile seemed to reach out to touch him and he
felt something flip-flop inside. By God, he was
thinking, between Felicia Ziegler and Sally Ellinger, Doc Golightly had to be crazy if he thought
Slocum was hitting the trail.

From the window of Sister Ellie's house, the two
men watched Slocum and Billy Ellinger riding out
of town.

"It is him."

"That's what I know."

As the two riders moved farther down the street
in the setting sunlight, the two men moved closer
to the window, their eyes following the receding
figures.

"But how do you know he's working for
Ellinger?" asked the first speaker, a thin man with
a grey derby hat sitting squarely on top of his head.
His intense, bony face looked like it had been shel-
lacked, while the Texas longhorn mustache seemed
to have been pasted on. He was very thin, there

was a lot of air between his galluses and his little
chest, and the big hogleg at his hip looked like it
was about all he could carry. Harry Poon was a
known lunger; indeed, he'd come West on doctor's
orders to get rid of the consumption, but he had
thrived, mostly by killing gambling adversaries.
His favorite pastime besides drinking, fornicating,
gambling, and "killing fools," was quoting. He was
past his prime now—everyone knew it—but none
said so, for he could still pull a trigger. Yet the old
tiger had lost his fangs. He was gathering history,
and it would be only a matter of time before some
young kid built his reputation on dispatching the
famous Harry Poon. But meanwhile, there was no
waiting line to try him out.

His companion was a big man wearing a hickory
shirt that was torn in three places. He was sucking
on a wooden lucifer. His face was covered by a red
beard, his hands were huge, with long red hair on
the backs of them; though at present his left hand
was under a bandage thanks to John Slocum's Colt.
His nose had been broken more than once, and he
had a scar running from just below his left ear down
into the collar of his shirt, where it disappeared.
Some people on first meeting Hammerhead Hogan,
a former shotgun guard for Wells Fargo, wondered
just how far down that scar ran, but nobody ever
asked.

"I could drop him easy from here with that
Winchester of yours," Hammerhead said.

"I will take care of that." Harry Poon's words
were flecked with annoyance, and Hammerhead
Hogan, who could have crunched the little man in

one bare hand, took a step to the side. Poon was
no man to mess with, and as he saw the gleam come
into the gunman's eyes he felt something slice
through his guts. Fortunately, Harry didn't pursue
his irritation. Has-been he might be, Hammerhead
was thinking, but the son of a bitch could strike
that hogleg like a rattler's tongue. He'd seen it.
He'd seen him shooting swinging bottles the other
day, showing some of the boys how to finger their
aim. It had been mighty impressive.

To change the subject, Hammerhead said, "Tell
me about Slocum. He is tough; that I know—but
what else?"

"I have heard tell he is part Injun. For sure, he
don't forget nothing, and he can read trail sign with
the best of 'em. They tell that he rode with Quantrill.
I don't know if that is so but, knowing him, how
he is, it don't matter. He is mean enough to have
ridden with Lucifer."

"Who?" Hammerhead's big streaked eyeballs
bugged out of his big red head.

"The devil, you dumb shit," snapped Harry Poon.
"So it don't matter whether it is true or not. He is
a mean son of a bitch, and the sooner the quicker
to be done with him the better."

"What about Hampton?" Hammerhead asked,
changing the subject. "Ain't we working for them?"
And he began scratching inside his ear with the
wooden lucifer.

"You are working for me, Hogan. Do not forget
that."

"Sure."

"And I will take care of Slocum. Don't you forget that either! We have an old score to settle," he concluded solemnly. His somber eyes half-closed as his lips moved. Yet the words were audible.

"'Tis time, my adversary, 'tis time. Sweet death awaits..."

# 4

"I'll be pulling out," he told the girl after they'd had supper that night and Billy was in bed. "I want to thank you for everything you've done."

She had just taken out her knitting bag and was preparing to continue on the sweater she had started a few nights before.

"We will be sorry to see you go, Slocum, Billy and I. You are welcome to stay."

He thought he caught a slight tremor in her voice, but he couldn't be sure. She had her eyes on her work, and he couldn't tell what expression was on her face.

In the silence that fell upon them he watched her hands working. Presently she looked up at him. "Are you planning on leaving the country, the Basin?"

"Not much to stay here for," he countered. "I figure the man who was following me, if he's still about, can pick up my trail again, and it won't be any hassle for you and Billy."

"We don't consider it a hassle."

He grinned at her, and then his eyes fell to her bosom, which he found particularly attractive this evening. "I know. But it's time for me to move on," he told her.

She laid down her knitting and regarded him for a moment with her hands lying loosely in her lap. "You really are a man of the trail, aren't you?"

"You could put it that way."

"You live a very exciting life."

"I like it. There's something close to . . . I don't know what . . . something." And he watched her face soften.

"I think I understand you," she said, and picked up her knitting. But her hands didn't start to work for a moment, and then when they did begin she started to speak. "There's something else, though, isn't there? I know how Dr. Golightly talks. In a way," and she was smiling gently, "in a way he's our local newspaper. I've a strong feeling he may have mentioned some things to you."

"With perceptions like yours, young lady, you'd do pretty damn well on the trail, I'd say."

And though she didn't look up from her busy hands, he saw the smile coming into her face.

"I see."

"But that has nothing to do with my leaving."

"I know it hasn't." She looked up. "You're not

that sort. But, you know, it's good to have things straight between people."

"It's not been easy for you," Slocum said gently.

A moment passed. "It's my life," she said.

"People are cruel."

"They can be. They aren't always."

"Right." And then, "You say you wish I'd stay. Maybe you ought to hit the trail, too. You and Billy."

She smiled fully at him now. "Maybe we'd run into you one day."

And once again he appreciated how very sharp she was. She didn't miss a thing.

For a moment, both of them listened to the choppy bark of a coyote coming through the night.

"I figure, too, if I'm a target, then you and Billy will also be targets." And as he said it, he realized why that particular thought had come. "That was no coyote," he said.

Just at that moment they heard the horses pounding in. Slocum was already on his feet, while she had reached out and turned down the lamp, dropping the room into darkness.

"Get into your room, with Billy," he said, loosening the hammer thong on the Colt as he stepped to the side of the cabin door.

The hammering on the door was from a gun butt. "Slocum!"

He noticed that the girl didn't move. "Billy's already up," she said in a low voice.

"What do you want?" Immediately after speaking, Slocum moved from where he'd been standing, just in case the visitors decided to throw lead at the sound of his voice.

"You've got till tomorrow noon to get out of the country. You hear me? Noon tomorrer you be shut of Sunshine Basin, or you'll be staying here permanent!"

He heard Sally moving beside him as Billy slipped into the darkened room. The men outside were not at all quiet. He could hear them talking amongst themselves, and even heard some of their bodily movements as they clomped onto the porch of the house or spoke to their horses. It was clear that they'd been drinking.

Softly he said to the girl, "I want you to talk to them. Distract them."

"You're not going outside!" Her alarm caused her to raise her voice, and he reached out and touched her.

Aloud he called out, "I hear you, mister. I'll think it over." He started to move swiftly to the back of the cabin and into the kitchen.

"There is no thinking it over, Slocum! You get out of this country by noon tomorrow!" The voice was as hard as a gun barrel.

As he slid out the kitchen window, he heard the girl's voice talking to the men, though it wasn't clear what she was saying. He was wondering whether the visit had been planned or whether it was just a fun-and-frolic caper spurred by liquor. At least they hadn't come in shooting.

Hugging the log wall of the back of the cabin, he slipped along to the corner and moved up toward the front, where there was a rain barrel offering good cover. There was a moon, though it was not easy to see beyond a few feet. He could make out the men at the door, and behind them their horses, but no detail.

"Sally, you stay out of this!" The voice was angry. Slocum knew the signs. It wouldn't take much for the man to prod himself into action, especially with a woman coming onto the scene.

Slocum lifted the Winchester .44-.40 and sighted around the side of the barrel.

"I have got you covered with this cut-down Greener. Don't even think of moving!"

They had already frozen.

"Now get this: I am leaving here when I get damn good and ready. And not until. Now get on your horses and haul ass! I mean right now!"

"Slocum..." The voice had lost its hard ring, and the speaker never got to the rest of what he might have been going to say.

"One funny move, mister, and there'll be nothing left of you but your ankles!"

As they rode out he watched, not moving. There were four of them. The moon was clear of any clouds now, and he could see the riders distinctly.

She was waiting inside the back door as he entered.

"It was Burt Hampton," she said.

"Let's have a light." And when the coal-oil lamp had been lighted, he looked at her and at the boy standing beside her.

"Gee, Slocum, you really sent them packing!"

Billy's voice was pulsing with admiration and excitement. His sister, on the other hand, looked and sounded somber.

"Will they come back, do you think?" she asked.

"I'll be gone. Like I told you." And he smiled at her. "Billy, you'd better get to bed." He turned to the girl. "And you, too. See you in the morning."

But she didn't go into her room, just stayed waiting near him as they both heard Billy climbing into his bedroll. "'Night," he called.

"Where will you go?" she asked after a short silence.

He didn't answer her. He was listening, his head a little to the side, his eyes half closed.

She waited, listening with him.

"You got any lucifers?" he asked.

When she handed him some, he put them in his shirt pocket.

"You're going out again?" she asked as he checked his handgun.

He nodded. "You bar the door and don't open it for anyone except me. I'll go out the kitchen window."

The moon was more clear for the few clouds that had obstructed it earlier were gone. He was glad to find that he could move more quickly than before. Swiftly he picked up the tracks of the Hampton horses leaving, and now found those they'd made coming in. He didn't really need the lucifers. He took one now and put the clean end into his mouth. Chewing it helped him think.

Down by the round horse corral he found what he was looking for: the tracks of the fifth horse that

had ridden in with the Hamptons but had not ridden
out. They led through the corral to the barn.

Now it was difficult, for the full light of the
moon was spreading over the ranch. And so he
waited. It must have been an hour later, according
to his reckoning, that the moon faded behind a thin
cloud, and for a few moments the approach to the
barn was not so visible. Swiftly he ran around the
corral and came up on the side of the log structure.

Leaning against the big logs, he listened. Nothing. When he moved nearer to the door, he heard
it then: the low whiffle of a horse and the jingle
and creek of saddle rigging and a bridle.

The moon was down when after a long wait he
heard the barn door open. The man was leading a
small cow pony, and in his left hand he was carrying
a long gun. When he tied the horse to the corral
gate and started in the direction of the cabin, it
became clear what his intention was.

"Hold it right there, mister."

The man stopped dead in his tracks.

"Drop the rifle, and unbuckle."

He was a stocky little man with a full head of
hair, a battered hat, and a Texas mustache. He moved
like a man in those middle years which for some
people last a long time.

"Now take off your clothes."

"What the hell!"

"Your coat, hat, shirt, and your pants. All of it."

"For Christ's sake, Slocum!"

"Know my name, huh?"

"So what if I do?" The tone was sulky now, but
he had started to unbutton his clothes, and soon he

had shucked off coat and shirt.

"Your boots."

"Son of a bitch!"

"What's that?"

"Not you, for Christ's sake. I was just cussin'."
He stood there now in his longhandles, his woolen
underwear, with the crotch sagging down between
his knobby legs.

"Now you get on that horse and git, and don't
ever come back."

"I'll be back, Slocum. You can go fuck yerself.
I'll be back. Count on it."

Slocum let a sigh run through his whole body.
"Clowns like you never learn, do you?" He moved
over to the horse, signaling his prisoner to move
away a few paces. Then, one-handed, he uncinched
the belly band and let the saddle dump onto the
ground. When he slapped the horse on his rump,
he took a step away from the saddle.

"Get that jug over yonder by the corner of the
barn." He pointed with the barrel of the Colt.

And when the man brought it, Slocum said, "Put
it down there and turn around and sit."

"This what they did when you was with
Quantrill?"

Suddenly the Colt was back in its holster and
the prisoner was flat on his back, backhanded by
Slocum, the blood running from his smashed nose
and mouth. In a flash, Slocum had the handgun out
again. "That's for your bad manners." He stood
watching the man struggle painfully to his feet.
"You do give me a idea. Take off them longhandles."

"What the hell for?"

"I said take 'em off."

When he was naked, Slocum holstered the pistol and picked up the jug.

"Slocum, you wouldn't do that!" The man took a step backward as he started to shake, his eyes widening in fear. "That there is coal oil! You wouldn't . . . !"

"Thought you wanted me to show you how Quantrill and Bloody Bill Anderson and the boys did it, you son of a bitch." And, taking a step forward, he splashed the coal oil on the other's naked body.

"Now, you son of a bitch, you get on that animal and ride; he's got a good, sharp back so you can break your balls. Make tracks 'fore I decide to light you!"

He watched the shaking man clamber onto the pony's bare back and slide off. Then he tried again and made it. Slocum smacked his hat at the horse's rump and he began a fast canter with his rider bouncing up and down, crying out and trying with his free hand to protect his genitals.

Sally was awake when Slocum reached the house and entered quietly through the kitchen window. Seated in the armchair where she had been knitting the evening before, she rose and almost stumbled as she came toward him, her hair in disarray, her face pale with concern.

"Slocum . . ."

"I feel great," he said with a big grin as his arms encircled her, and he felt her soft body melting against him.

"Is Billy asleep?"

"He must be."

He bent and lifted her and started to carry her across the room.

"Where are you taking me?"

"To bed. Can you think of a better place?"

He had placed her gently on the bed and turned back to close her bedroom door. When he returned to her she was already undressing. And in only a moment her full breasts bounced out of her chemise and into his hands. The nipples were large, the breasts young and delightfully springy under his caress. He bent his head and took one in his mouth as a shudder shook her.

"Get your clothes off," she whispered.

He was already undressing, and now she was helping him, unbuttoning his trousers and reaching in to grab his erection.

"My God, it's big!" she gasped. And her delight thrilled him.

In another moment they were both naked. She had both hands on his huge member, stroking it as she brought it between her spread legs.

"Oh, God, Slocum. How I have wanted you! Please, dear, please give it. Give it!"

"It's right here, and it's ready."

With one hand now she reached up and brought his head and lips to her breasts again. "God, chew them! Suck them!" And Slocum was only too happy to please.

Now she took his great cock in both hands and rubbed its head into her soaking pubic brush while

he lifted his face from her breasts and sank his
tongue deep into her mouth. At the same time he
slipped the tip of his organ into her creamy lips,
but not far; teasing, tantalizing, until at last she
cried out, begging for more.

"Come in, dear! Come in!" And she grabbed his
buttocks, bringing him into her, as her legs spread
wider and his great shaft plunged down and then
up into her until she almost cried out.

"My God, My God, what are you doing to me
with that huge thing!" she whimpered.

Now he was fully in her and they began a sinuous
riding together.

"Stroke! Stroke!" Her whisper was almost a cry.

Now he drew almost completely out, then slowly
slid back down and up, then increasing his speed,
while she matched him.

Reaching down with both hands she grabbed his
balls which had been banging against her buttocks,
soaking with their mixed fluids.

"I can't stand it," she whispered. "I can't stand
it! Come! Dear God, come, come with me . . . come
. . . come . . . come!"

But he delayed, drawing the exquisite moment
to the point where it was hardly endurable. And
then, as their bodies rode faster and faster, plunging
and bucking now while she drew her long legs up
onto his shoulders so that she was almost lying on
the back of her neck, her legs high up and around
him as she gripped his pounding buttocks, while he
stroked deeper and deeper, higher and higher, until
she was gasping and crying.

"Faster. Oh, my God, faster!" And they were

racing until at length their whipping bodies became one as they exploded together and she cried in his ear, "You're drowning me. It's like a great fountain!"

They lay there exhausted with joy, their thighs and bellies soaking. She nestled in his arms, murmuring, her breath hot on his shoulder, while he lay his thigh across her.

But not for long.

Soon her fingers began to play between his legs and he was again erect and this time she bent down, pumping him with her fist as she took his great head in her mouth and then slid her lips along his shaft until she was nearly choking. At the point where neither of them could endure it any longer he took it out and, spreading her legs wide with his own, plunged his throbbing manhood into her soft, quivering vagina, and together they instantly found their rhythm driving their avid bodies to the ultimate joy as they exploded again and again.

Slocum had been shoeing the crazy white mare that Billy and his sister used for a workhorse. She was a gaunt animal, yet tough as an enforced spinster, with a blind right eye. Billy held her halter up close while Slocum did the shoeing. The two carried on an active silence between them, interspersed with occasional questions from the boy, mostly on the art of blacksmithing.

"Gee, Slocum, you sure know a lot!" The boy's admiration broke forth in spite of himself.

Slocum, with the mare's left forefoot between his legs while he quickly nailed on the shoe, grunted.

And in a moment he said, "It don't hurt to know everything," speaking around the nails he held in his mouth.

The mare was spooky. She always had been. Someone must have beaten her a lot about the head at some -time. There were times when you just couldn't touch her. She jumped at everything and at nothing. Once she dragged her foot between Slocum's legs and but for the leather chaps he was using as a protective apron, she'd have sliced right into his thigh with the nails he hadn't yet clinched.

"Hold her tight now, and stay close to her," he told the boy.

He was finally finished. Now he told Billy to lead her into the barn, snub her tight to the hay bin in her stall, and then roach her mane so it wouldn't get fouled in harness when they worked her.

He stood with a lighted quirly in his mouth, watching the boy lead the mare into the barn. The smoke of the quirly hung nicely in the crisp morning air, which he knew would heat up shortly. He felt good. Ever since he'd sent the Hampton boys packing the night before he had felt really good. And it had been good shoeing the mare.

He had just lifted his head to squint at the weather from beneath the wide brim of his Stetson when he heard the white mare whinny almost into a scream, followed by the crash of timber in the barn. Before he took two steps the mare was backing out of the doorway, her ears flat down along her neck in fury and fear, with Billy hanging around her neck, his arms as tight as he could make them, and with the wooden bar of the manger bouncing along behind the boy on the end of the halter rope. Crazy with fear, she was trying to raise up on her hind legs to strike the boy with her front hooves.

"Stay close," Slocum told him, backing away in order not to spook the mare any more. "Don't let go or she'll kick you!"

Billy was tight against her, so she couldn't reach him with her striking hooves. She backed all the way out of the barn, dragging the boy and the cross-piece from the manger with her.

Dragging him into the middle of the round corral, she now tried to shake him off by spinning and rearing, but the boy held fast to her neck. At last she stood rigid, forelegs planted wide, sides heaving, and good eye bloodshot and rolling, and waited.

Slocum said nothing; he didn't move.

Billy brought his arms down very slowly. Carefully he reached for the halter and slid his hand down the rope to the piece of the manger. He untied the rope. Slocum saw that the boy's legs were shaking as he stood close to the mare and talked to her softly. It seemed a very long time before her terror began to leave. He patted her neck and her shoulder, stroked her softly between her eyes. At last she bent her head toward him a little, still snorting suspiciously, but with her ears up now and a little to the side, questioning.

The boy felt her hot, nervous breath on the palms of his hands as he caressed her wet muzzle.

"Looks like you grabbed yourself a handful of horse there," Slocum said, and the boy grinned sheepishly.

"Well, you said to roach her mane."

"Put her back in the barn," Slocum said, "And we'll see what this feller is after." He was looking east toward the rider who had just come up out of a draw and was cantering toward them.

"It's Uncle Cole," Billy said, and Slocum caught the note of excitement.

"Get the mare in the barn," Slocum told him. "You can finish the roaching later."

Cole Ellinger was a man of few words. Doc Golightly, in describing the cattleman, was not above using the worn expression, ". . . and he uses them few damn seldom." Cole, a man of average height, gave the impression of greater size, due to an innate dignity which the swiftly mounting hostilities in Sunshine Basin had so far been unable to diminish.

His response to the news of the Hamptons riding out to his favorite niece's cabin in the middle of the night to issue threats was instant. He turned slightly dark with controlled anger, finished his cup of coffee, then saddled his big dun gelding, a fine cutting horse, and rode out to the Double E. The sun wasn't long up when he came around the low-cut bank by Harms Creek and saw the figures in the round horse corral.

Now he stood facing the man he'd been hearing about, the man who to a lot of people seemed all height and width, and who moved with a grace and suppleness more Indian than white, more animal than human. Cole found it easy to see why the Hamptons wanted to be shut of him, especially when he looked into John Slocum's green eyes. Those eyes were a shock to a lot of people. They said nothing; they simply looked. They held the solemnity of a child and a sage. Cole Ellinger had met many men of all kinds; he himself was known as a tough man and a fair one, a man you didn't try to rinky-dink. Cole didn't have much use for most of the men he'd run into in his lifetime, but here was someone different. And for a moment Cole Ellinger felt an uneasiness he hadn't known since he was a shaver. But the moment passed with the trace of a smile that came into his own grey eyes as he nodded to the man who stood there calmly looking at him plumb center.

At that moment Billy came out of the barn, and the tableau was broken as Ellinger and his nephew greeted each other.

"Billy, I want to have a word with Mr. Slocum here. Why don't you go on up and tell Sally I'll be looking forward to some coffee and biscuits."

Both men turned their heads to watch the boy running to the house with his news.

And now, like western men always did from the very beginning, the two squatted in the corral, studying whatever was in front of them from beneath the brims of their Stetson hats.

"I got wind of the Hamptons paying a call," Cole said.

"They come by for a spell."

"I understand they told you to get out of the country."

Slocum tipped his hat back a little on his head. "That's what I got from the conversation, too."

"I see you are still here."

"I never did like doing what people told me," Slocum said.

Cole Ellinger took a cigar out of his shirt pocket. "It's a good Havana," he said, offering it.

Slocum nodded as he took the cigar while Ellinger brought out another for himself. In the moment of pleased silence that followed each man sniffed the tobacco, bit the little bullet off the end of his cigar, and lighted. The blue smoke rose above their bent heads as they remained hunkered in the corral.

Presently, Slocum took the cigar out of his mouth and studied the ash. "Good enough," he said. "What can I do for you, Mr. Ellinger?"

Cole Ellinger liked that. "I want you to come work with me."

"Doing what?"

"I figure you're pretty well up on what's going on in the Basin. It's getting out of hand, and it's been going on too damn long. But the Hamptons won't listen to reason, and they've gone and hired some gunmen."

"And you figure to even it out."

"Something like that. Only it ain't just your gun, Slocum."

"Some people say I rode with Quantrill—people that don't know what they're talking about, or how to keep their mouths shut."

"I'd heard that. But that isn't why I'm offering you a job." And then he added, "It's not why I'm asking."

Slocum appreciated the careful admission. "Why, then?"

"I see the way you are with Billy. I didn't want to hire you on, but some of the men did, as a gun. When I rode out here this morning I still didn't really want to, but I knew we needed you as a gun. Now I'm asking you different." And he looked square at Slocum.

"I'll turn it over," Slocum said. "Give it a day." He paused, running the palm of his hand along the side of his jaw.

"I take it you ain't working for anybody right now," Ellinger said.

"I never work for anybody excepting myself."

The two men stood now, checking the sky, the weather.

"Then I'll get word from you . . . maybe tomorrow," Ellinger said.

Slocum nodded and the cattleman started toward the house as they both saw Sally come out onto the porch and wave.

Slocum said, "The guns the Hamptons hired; they have got names?"

Ellinger had stopped and turned back to him. "I don't know offhand, no. Did hear one name, though; someone named Spoon, something like that."

"Good enough." Slocum turned toward the barn. "I'll just check the mare. Then maybe I'll see you all directly for some of those biscuits."

And as he walked into the barn he was thinking of Forth Worth and Harry Poon. Only he knew it wasn't Harry Poon following him, trying to dry-gulch him. Poon could never have handled a trail in the mountains like that. But Poon might be connected with the man who had shot him. In any case, it was going to be interesting. The score with the drygulcher, the score with Harry Poon. Not to mention a little more scoring with Sally Ellinger.

# 5

The little bay horse wouldn't stand still, no matter how much Billy cussed him—under his breath, on account of the girl being there. He kept itching around trying to get a shot at Nan's blue roan with a rear hoof, and the roan kept backing off, scared. Then Billy got mad in spite of himself and gave the bay a couple of cuts across the rump with the reins.

"Kind of spooky, isn't he?" Nan said.

"He sure is. We come near losing each other a couple of times."

She laughed. She was wearing a check shirt, open at the throat and with the sleeves rolled up, and thin, washed-out Levi's with a hole in one knee. And she wore her brown hair down around her shoulders. Billy knew how soft it was; he'd touched

73

it once. Her eyes were hazel, and on her upper lip was a small freckle. She was a month and a day older than him.

He hadn't seen her in a long while, and now he didn't know what to say, nor did she. She was almost as shy as he was. They had known each other most of their lives, but it was only recently that something had changed; so it seemed to them, though neither one actively thought about it. Only neither the boy nor the girl felt they were "just thirteen," as their families would have put it.

Billy took the blade of grass out of his mouth and shook his hair out of his eyes. He grinned at the girl. He didn't know what to say; he just wanted to stay there forever looking at her.

Without a word they both started their horses back down the draw, walking the animals slowly, not talking, just riding softly through the day. He was glad the bay was behaving himself.

They rode pretty close—he saw to that, being bold all of a sudden—and now and again his knee brushed the roan. It felt good. And both of them listened to the sound of the river getting louder as they got closer to it. Then they came around the side of a low hill and could see the river, swollen and a dirty green and grey with the snow that was still melting in the mountains. Still without a word both drew rein and sat their horses and watched an uprooted tree go by in the water.

"It'll take Elmer Bergson's bridge out again," Nan said.

"Yeah . . . like last spring."

They crossed Elmer's bridge. It was pretty rickety. The bay acted real spooky and Billy thought for a minute maybe they wouldn't make it. In his mind he was already saving Nan from drowning, though he knew he didn't know how to swim.

Topping a low draw now they drew rein as the boy signaled; he was riding slightly ahead of her for the moment and now she drew abreast. His happy glance took in her soft, bright face, her shy smile as she returned his look. He was trying to figure how he could work the bay closer to her so that he could give her a kiss without being awkward, when suddenly he heard something. Drawing back, he saw she'd heard it, too.

A hollow, faint roaring that gradually kept getting louder. It was that strange mournful bellowing that comes from a herd of cattle forced along an unknown trail. As the two very young people listened the sound came clearly up the draw in the wind, faint, yet still coming nearer, and now growing more clear.

"It's cattle," he said. And without another word, as though by a signal from somewhere they began riding toward the sound, drawn by a magnet.

After some time they topped a low rise and reined in near a big clump of bullberry bushes where they could see the cattle were being held below in a draw.

"Wow!" the boy exclaimed. "I bet there's least a hundred head!"

"I'll bet it's more," she said, her breath catching with excitement.

"Maybe," Billy agreed.

"That's an awful lot of calves, it seems."

"And not many mothers. Can you see the brand?"

"No, I can't."

"I don't think there is any," he said. "See that fire?"

"They're going to brand them," she said, shielding her eyes to see better.

"But on the cows. There's only a few cows but they should have a brand," he insisted. "Say, isn't that your Grandpa down there?"

Suddenly he felt her silence beside him. When he turned he saw that her face had turned white.

"Billy . . ."

"What's the matter?"

A sob broke from her. "I've got to go home." And she turned the blue roan and kicked him into a gallop, and before he realized, she was too far away for him to follow.

This time when he looked back at the cattle he saw the Lazy Z brand, Barney Ziegler's Lazy Z on two of the cows, and for a minute he watched Hamp Hampton, sitting a big steeldust grey stud horse smoking a cigar.

Then he turned and looked again in the direction in which Nan Hampton had raced away.

He didn't follow her. He kicked the bay hard into a low canter, going right back the way they had come, gripping the reins so hard his knuckles were white, with his face shiny from tears of anger and futility.


"An' you let him whipsaw you?"

"Couldn't help it, Hamp," Clyde Hampton protested earnestly. "He was stashed back of that rain barrel with a goosegun, and he'd of cut us into a crowd quicker'n shit slippin' through a tin horn." Clyde looked at his brothers, Burt and Miles, for support.

"Dumb, riding up like that," snapped old Hamp. "Lettin' him know you were coming like that."

"Hamp, we figgered we'd throw a scare into him. We had no notion he was that slick."

Hamp Hampton had been walking back and forth in the cabin of the Hampton ranch, and now he stopped all at once. Stopped as though he'd been hit with something—a gnarled tree, seeded God knew when, suddenly struck by lightning; maybe the Finger of Jehovah. His huge red and yellow eyes fell upon his oldest son, Clyde. His mouth worked as though there was some bad taste in it. His hands moved, perhaps seeking help, or maybe searching breath. "Scare him? Scare John Slocum, you say?" A sigh like a file rubbing along a glass edge came from his pursed lips. "God Jesus Almighty! What assholes I have got for sons! Throw a scare in Slocum!" The great orbs turned from his offspring to the Above.

"Hamp, listen . . ."

"Paw . . . !"

The old man, sagging in his huge overalls, was struck dumb. Not for years, and only then in crisis, had a one of them resorted to that paternal designation. Paw! He stood looking at each one of them in turn, a drop of water right on the end of his long, bony nose, down which a noise rode loudly as though the old man was trying to eject some foreign body. Carefully he reached up and with his little finger

scratched deep into the nest of hair in his right ear.
Then, without pause, his gnarled hand swept to his
crotch and to his rear where his rusty fingers delved
pleasurably, seeking, and it seemed at last finding,
security.

"Got the goddamn fleas all about, damn it! Don't
you hooligans never take a bath?"

His eyes dropped to Old Crouch, the black and
white spotted dog who never left his side. Crouch
was part coyote, or maybe wolf, the old man maintained. And like all dogs that seldom bark—and
men, too—his bite was all the worse. He'd had
half an ear chewed off in a fight with a coyote, and
he was missing part of his tail, but he could wrangle
cattle, which was a lot tougher job than handling
sheep.

Old Hamp suddenly raised his forefinger; it
looked like a rusty spike. "You do not go getting
previous with a man like Slocum, by God! Don't
you assholes know anything? You damn fools is
just *askin'* to get your fool heads shot off. And did
you find out if he's working for Cole Ellinger? No!"
He roared out the answer to his own question,
clomping now around the cabin with a bottle of
whiskey he snatched by its neck from the table.

"And Tate! Where is he?"

"Told you, Paw." Miles almost whined the words,
but holding them close as though they were his,
like special cards, as though the fact of Cousin Tate
waiting in the barn to drygulch Slocum would re-
deem them totally in Hamp's eyes.

"Where is he then? He's had time aplenty to

shoot up Slocum! But I'll bet all three yore hairy
asses he is either been cold-cocked or killed—one—
by Slocum ere this moment!" He paused, licking
his lips, rooting into an armpit, his eyes on the dog
at his feet.

"Old Crouch there! Old Crouch has got more
sense in his left ball than you three knotheads got
in the whole of yez!" He snorted. "Tate waitin' in
the barn. Jesus! You ninnies!"

As he stomped around the cabin the light from
the two coal-oil lamps threw his shadow gro-
tesquely on the log wall. The old man didn't have
a beard and at the same time he was not clean-
shaven by any means. He was always in need of a
shave. How he maintained a two-three day growth
of beard without ever shaving mystified all.

Hamp Hampton was mysterious in more ways
than one. There were those who claimed he'd known
Lincoln. Others allowed that no self-respecting
president would be seen in such a one's company.
Actually, he'd been a drinking crony of Ulysses
Grant, and indeed now when in his liquor, which
was often, he would tell tall tales of his drinking
sessions with U.S.S. as he called him, new stories
created as he grew older. Old Hamp—and he'd
never allowed anyone in the family to forget it—
was an ordained minister. And he swore by the
Good Book. Yet, strangely, he had never insisted
that any of his sons or kin follow the way of the
Lord. Folks admired that.

He had walked to one of the windows now—it
was more like a porthole, really, through which one

could fire a rifle and yet be protected—and was looking out over the terrain as the evening began to fall over the country.

The Double H was situated in a blind sort of hole; you couldn't see the house till you were right on it. But those inside the house and nearby could see anyone riding up for quite a distance. And coming around the big butte and then down the low draw there was a track that cattle could follow easily enough. When the old man brought anything in there it wasn't likely to break out, not even horses. Hamp had been the first of any of the Hamptons— and preceding the Ellingers, too—to enter the Basin. Indeed, he had known The Town back in the days when the night riders had run it, when they'd buried their "permanent marshal" six feet down, and standing up in Main Street; for Marshal Zachary Entitle, when approached by outlaws with tempting offers and threats, had issued the interesting statement that he intended to stand on his own two feet and would take orders from no man. Hamp, it was said, was one of the frisky bunch who saw to it that when buried Marshal Zachary Entitle sure enough was still standing on his own two feet.

His boys were three, and all cut from the same bolt of cloth. Long on humor, short of temper, and totally self-centered; they loved the good things in life: money, whiskey, gambling, and women galore. The Town was just the place where they were able to exercise their fun. Even with the big ranchers around there'd been no problem. They rustled a few here and there, mostly from Barney Ziegler, but also from Tod Bendiller, Henry Wilson, and some others.

The boys were always telling themselves stories about old Hamp—that time he'd slickered Barney Ziegler when Barney rode over with a package of gunmen looking for some of his rustled stock. Barney had been real hard as he looked at Hamp and his three boys standing outside their cabin, and ordered—yes, by God, *ordered* Hamp to show him the hide belonging to that beef hanging from the tree back of the barn. Of course, Hamp never let any man order him, so the boys were all the more surprised when, meek as a kitten, Hamp said, "Why, sure, Barney, sure." Of course they knew too that the time the critter was butchered Hamp had them make the hide into a rope and before that was done he'd cut out the brand and dropped it into the fire.

Barney Ziegler saw a hide with the Hampton Double H on it, killed about two weeks back. He didn't know it had been taken off a cancered steer, and that Hamp had taken the trouble to stick him and bleed him before he took the hide off so it wouldn't look too dark.

The boys loved to tell that one—Barney Ziegler mad as a cat with his balls in turpentine, and Hamp was all honey: "Why, sure, Barney. Course, Barney," and all that sashayin' kind of talk. Hamp Hampton knew more tricks than a dozen Barney Zieglers could figure.

The only one who'd ever given him a hard time was Maw. They fought over his "shenanigans," as Maw—a beefy woman, hard-working and sober—

called his "little borrowings." But Hamp didn't mind belting her one now and again, after which he would give her the same old story: "You tend your own business. . . . There's plenty in this here country does the same as me. And them big outfits think a poor man ain't got the right to live. Well, to hell with them, I say. It's God's country and I'll put my brand on anything I see on this range that ain't mothered up. A maverick's a maverick, by God."

But Maw was dead now, taken by the croup, and so Hamp took it out on his sons. On the other hand, with his grandchildren and any young nephews and nieces he was the soul of kindness and a whole box of fun. His favorite was Nan; one of his former favorites had been Sally Ellinger. His boys—and others, too, including the Ellingers, who were now former kin and friends—had long since given up trying to figure him out.

The old man had been at the porthole a long time; the boys began to notice this. All three were in their thirties, but Clyde, Miles, and Burt had never gotten over their younger relationships with their father. All three were still wholly dependent on his favor. In consequence, they were the more deadly for having such a taskmaster to please.

"Well, I'll be a bung-eyed son of a bitch." The words broke ruefully from the old man, and in surprise, too.

"What's up, Hamp?"

"Gimme them glasses."

The field glasses were swiftly passed and the old man surveyed the sweeping land in front of the cabin.

"Holy shit!"

"Hamp, what d'you see?"

Their initial excitement now gave way to alarm as their sire turned to face them. For a moment he stood absolutely still—a preacher preparing to address his congregation—and then he began to shake.

"I knowed it! I knowed it!" He shook his head, and water sprang to his old eyes. And suddenly a great wheel of laughter rolled up his throat and out of his mouth. "You pismires! You clowns throw a scare into Slocum! You idiots! Here!" And he threw the field glasses at them; they were almost dropped as all three tried to catch them. "Take a look! Take a look, God damn you!" And he all but fell as his laughter increased and he started swaying around the room.

Suddenly he stood still and reached for the bottle. "God help me, siring such trash. Take a look! Take a look out that there winder at your cousin Tate, you stupid fools!"

And he looked down at Old Crouch, who was chewing at something in his paw, and shook his head knowingly.

For Slocum there were few places that could match it in the whole of the West. The snow would be there all summer, mantling the great peaks in dazzling white against the high blue sky. On the sides of the mountains, in the long green valleys, horses and cattle grazed, and in the tall timber and meadows there was game. The land was rich and it was clean. The days and nights were always new.

In the darkening now he lay on his bedroll on

the soft pine needles at the edge of the meadow, smelling the pine and fir and spruce, and whenever the wind stirred gently, the spotted saddle pony.

For a long time he lay quite still, not doing anything with it, trying only to accommodate this taste of peace, of harmony from which he had been lost. In this way he fell quietly asleep.

At dawn he awakened as imperceptibly as he had fallen asleep. He waited, his mind tranquil, watching the first rays of the sun, itself not yet visible, tinting the cloudless sky. And he knew that harmony in him still, that motion inside that was also a stillness.

And he lay there listening to it; so infinitely stronger than anything imagined that it was almost, not quite unbearable; like sound, like a chord striking through his whole body.

He rose and rolled his bedding. Now the sun was just at those distant mountains, stroking the quiet sky. For several moments he simply stood there listening to the life of the meadow, feeling the world. Now the morning sun filled the meadow with warmth and gold.

He built a small fire, using scraps of spruce and pine, and then he boiled coffee. With it he ate some of Sally Ellinger's baking-powder biscuits. He had a second cup of coffee, loath to leave the pastoral scene. For yet another moment he lingered, watching an eagle swing high overhead, then dive to a rocky cliff, landing out of sight. Slocum stood up, scattered the fire, checked his horse's rigging, and in a few moments he had led him out of the meadow and through the timber to the cabin.

Sally had told him of the cabin at Jack Creek and he had decided to move there, since he would surely attract trouble for the girl and her brother if he remained at the Double E. The cabin wasn't far from the Ellingers', yet it was high up and well protected from the casual trail rider, in a small clearing in the timber.

Slocum had deliberately slept in the meadow the night before in case anyone had taken the notion to track him. He didn't want to be caught indoors, no matter how solid the structure. And indeed, he decided that he would spend his nights outside the cabin from now on. Anyway, he preferred sleeping under the sky, and waking to the feel of the sun.

For a good while he remained in the cover of the trees, studying the building to make sure it was not inhabited. Finally satisfied, he tied his horse in the timber and walked around the perimeter of the clearing looking for signs of any visitors. But there was nothing, and by the time he returned to his horse he was satisfied.

The cabin was a low one-room structure built of spruce, with a flat sod roof. It had been solidly built against the mountain winter. The logs, he noted with approval, were at least eight inches in diameter, straight, and not tapering. Whoever had built the cabin had done a tight job, coping rather than notching the ends of each log so that it fitted tightly over the log below it. This, as far as he was concerned, was better than cutting square notches which, unless done with extreme care, could still admit water and cold air. On the outside the builder had used mud and manure for chinking between the logs, and on the inside, strips of wood. Inside, the job was not as careful; someone else had done it. The floor was dirt, the roof was flat, the sod supported by thin though sturdy logs. But it was snug. There was a window, a small aperture with a removable piece of wood, that when in place released no light to the outside. And so there was privacy. In one corner stood a jumbo stove. And there were supplies of salt, flour, coffee, and other staples, and, most important, firewood.

These cabins were not uncommon in the mountains, usually built by trappers for the traveler rather than as a home for any one person or family. They were landmarks in a certain sense, places of refuge for travelers to spend a night or two. Besides, it was the unwritten law that the traveler would not go without cutting a supply of firewood for the next person, leaving supplies in trade for what he had used. Frequently, too, those who stopped by worked on the cabin, putting up shelves, repairing the chinking, or working on the sod roof.

The cabin was on the north side of Jack Creek, not far from Sunshine Basin. It would be the ideal place for him, Slocum realized. It was accessible, but not easily so. His main plan was to move on now that his body had mended, and even though he was surely enjoying the pleasures of Sally Ellinger's bed, he felt it was no time to get involved in some family quarrel which, as Doc Golightly put it in his quaint expressiveness, "was monumenting into a chaos!"

Jack Creek would be the place where he could wait for whoever was tracking him. He was not impatient, but he wanted to get it over with. In the Ellinger cabin with the girl and boy, he was definitely hampered; moreover, there was the likelihood that whoever was after him would try to get at him through the two Ellingers. Here, alone, he could even take the initiative now that he was mended. Good enough. And then . . . then he'd move on.

He had seen that parting had not been easy for Sally, yet she'd kept it clean. "Come by when you've a notion," she'd said.

He'd not told her where he was going; there was always the possibility that someone might get it out of her, perhaps by using the boy. And so he'd said nothing of his plans, whether he would still be around or was leaving the country for good.

"I'll come see you again," he said. "I've a notion we'll meet again."

"As you wish, Slocum. You are always welcome." And she had looked deep into his eyes. He could feel the pull; it was as though she was not looking at him with her eyes at all, but rather looking at him from someplace deep inside herself. It was a special feeling, a feeling he'd experienced only with one or two older Indians he had known years ago.

There was a makeshift corral next to the cabin, and he led his horse in and stripped him. He rubbed him down, taking his time, always with his listening in the surrounding timber, and now and again stopping his work to take a look around. Then he grained the pony and inspected the corral. It needed some repair, and he spent the rest of the morning securing the poles and posts.

The cabin was neat, with everything he required. It was good being on the trail again. He would miss the girl; but then, at the Ellinger ranch he had missed the trail. The paradox brought a wry smile to his face.

He spent the afternoon cleaning his guns, the Colt Peacemaker .44-.40 and the Winchester rifle which chambered the same bullet. Afterward, he made some repairs on the cabin chinking. Then he walked to the meadow. In the late afternoon, the dying sunlight was warm on the green meadow grass. He stood there, taking it in, hearing the slight sighing of the trees. High up, the cool and the dark were coming, and he felt it in his shoulders, his hands, while far below in the valley it was still light. He listened to the life of the meadow, watched the bright sunlight touching the blades of grass, and now his eyes found the snowy peaks of the distant mountains.

That night he cooked his evening meal in the meadow. After dark he moved to another place near a stand of high spruce, and unrolled his bedding. He slept fully clothed with his Colt in his hand.

The next morning, after checking that no one had been near the cabin during the night, he saddled the spotted pony and rode down the mountain toward the town.

In the back room of the Hard Winter Saloon six men sat around a baize-topped table that had seen better times. These were all members of the Ellinger family; while they headquartered north of The Town, this day for some reason or other, they had decided to meet at the Hard Winter.

When Cole Ellinger entered the room, the six at the table turned their attention fully upon him.

"Well Cole." The short man with the patchy-looking beard poured a glass of whiskey for the new arrival. "What do you bring?"

"Slocum has pulled out."

Almost everybody at the table stirred at this piece of news.

"You mean, left the country?" A man with somber eyes and a pitted nose lifted his glass, his eyes on his cousin.

"I don't know if he's plumb left, Sam. Let's face it, he's a drifter, though a good man." And Cole held up his hand with the palm out to stem any possible adverse interpretation of his words. "But still not a man to settle." And then he added, "Hell, it's not his fight."

A smile or two drifted through the group, but carefully; yet Tim Ellinger, bolder than the rest, said, "And Cousin Sally maybe regrets it?" And then, swiftly covering, as he saw the cloud on Cole's face, "I'm saying that with her best interests at heart, Cole. But she needs a man out there. Billy's a great boy, as we all know, but I for one am concerned about the two of them out there at the edge of things all alone."

"So am I." Cole put down his glass.

Art Miller, a short man with a cast in his eye, spoke next. "But they're not involved, is how I see it—Sal and her brother."

"They are involved, Art, whether they like it or not," Cole insisted. "You've been down in Piney

Creek; you're not up on the latest. The Hamptons
are aiming to drive their stock up onto the mountain
soon as they get done branding. And they want to
take 'em right through the Double E. Ziegler's closed
the Ten Fork route, and Hamp Hampton wants a
shorter route anyway."

Big Bill Fletcher, another cousin to everyone
present, added, "Sally's been told, Art, but she
won't move into town or with any of us. She's
stubborn, you know. Just like Harry, her father."

"So what are we going to do?" Cole Ellinger
leaned back in his chair, keeping his arms straight
out, the palms of his hands flat on the baize top.

"You say you spoke with Slocum?" Tod
Greenough asked, his left eyelid dropping as he
regarded his brother-in-law.

"I offered him to come sign up with us. He
wasn't interested. Said it was a family affair—
something like that."

"Did you offer him money?"

"I did. I brought it up when we all had coffee
out to the Double E. He was still hard in his no."

"But did you point out to him that Hamp has
hired gunmen? It's no family thing any more."

"It is for the likes of Burt Hampton, I'll wager."
Tim Ellinger's deep voice rolled over the table.

"Let's drop that," Cole said, without turning his
head.

"Didn't mean it like it sounds, Cole. Only..."

"I said we'll drop it."

Silence fell like a stone in the room, which by
now was thick with tobacco smoke, the smell of
whiskey and men. They were seated near the jumbo

stove, which was out, it being spring. Nevertheless, the men were partly turned to it, being still somewhat in their winter ways, looking to the stove for something it was no longer giving. Tod Greenough let fly a thick stream of tobacco juice and saliva, which hit the side of the stove. And there was a pause in the conversation, a little opening, as though the company were waiting for the hiss and sizzle the liquid would have made in winter with the fire going.

"Shit," Tod said, his eyelid seeming to droop even more. The single word fell aimlessly in the tight little room.

It was Cole Ellinger who took up the line of conversation. "No matter; he has turned us down."

Bill Fletcher now spoke. "I am surprised, Cole."

"At what?"

"At your wanting to hire a gunman. All along, it's been yourself against the guns. And because of you the Hamptons have gotten away with murder. How come you've changed your mind?"

"I wasn't changing my mind. I wanted to hire Slocum as a ramrod, a man who gets things done, and also as a protector for Sal and Billy."

"And he still turned you down?"

Cole Ellinger nodded.

"And to throw a scare into Hamp?" Roy Ellinger, scratching his patchy beard, asked shrewdly; he was a very short man, speaking from the vicinity of Bill Fletcher's fat elbow, which was leaning on the table very close to the speaker's glass of whiskey.

Cole didn't answer. His eyes moved slowly around the circle of faces. All were family, either direct or through marriage. "I do not see a single gunman here in this lot," he said. "And the Hampton boys don't neither. You can bet on that. And let's get one thing straight." His eyes bored into Bill Fletcher. "I did not refuse to go gunning for the Hamptons because of not wanting to shoot every last one of the sons of bitches, but because I am not so goddamn stupid as to go up against that bunch. You all know the same as me that, hired guns or not, the Hamptons are killers, every one. We ain't. We'd fight; I don't doubt any man's courage at this table. But we are not like them. We're cattlemen, not rustlers and gunhawks. And I for one do not want my wife or kids shot up. Which will surely happen if we ain't by God goddamn careful!"

"Come on, Cole," Tod Greenough chided. "You know, and we all know, we've done our share with the hot iron. We're family here. Let's be honest about it. I am saying I have branded my share of slicks, and so has everyone else at this table."

A ponderous silence followed this interesting statement. Cole Ellinger finally looked up from his glass. "Tod, that is so. And so have I. So have ninety percent of the cattlemen in the West. We all know that. That's what we were all of us doing with Hamp and his crowd when we first come out here. But it is different now. Even Barney Ziegler never minded losing a few calves to an iron here and there—I'm speaking of unbranded stuff, slicks. But Hamp, he's been using a running iron and changing brands. That is different, by God!" And he brought his big fist down on the table with a bang, shaking a couple of drinks pretty badly, so that their owners reached out swiftly in alarm.

"He has done it to us. Ain't that how this whole goddamn fight started, for Christ's sake. Don't a one of you remember? He switched the Double E to a Double H. Only Harry caught on to it!" He glared at all of them in turn.

"Cole, take it slow, man." It was Roy Ellinger, scratching his patchy beard.

In the short silence that followed someone belched and Bill Fletcher moved his ponderous elbow, coming within an ace of knocking over Cousin Roy's whiskey, but yet not even noticing.

"But let us stick closer to the point," Cole Ellinger said, and some of those present caught the urgency in his voice.

"What are you driving at, Cole?"

"Like Hampton driving his herd to the mountain. He's grown his herd a good bit since last spring, and we all know he wants to push 'em right through the Double E; save all that time."

"And us, too," someone said. "But we are satisfied to go by Ten Fork. Is that what you're telling us, Cole?"

"I am saying that we have got to do something about Hamp pushing his herd through the Double E, if indeed he aims to go that far."

"Then we should get somebody like Slocum."

"Or handle it ourselves."

"Hamp Hampton gets up on that mountain, he'll get the best range, that's a gut. He'll be up there first is what I am saying."

Cole Ellinger stood up, his six feet almost reach-

ing to the coal-oil lamp that hung from the ceiling.
"What are we going to do? We'll do what we can.
I am not hiring a professional gunman."

"Cole, we've got to arm up. Only language the
Hamptons will listen to is gun talk!" Bill Fletcher
slapped his big hand down hard on the baize-top
table.

"No." Cole Ellinger seemed to stand even taller.
"No!"

In the sparkling light he rode the spotted pony along
the narrow deer trail just under the rimrocks, easing
down through the timber, now past a cluster of
mountain lilies. It was slow going. The trail was
as hard as iron, with now and again slippery footing. The horse picked its way slowly, always careful
with his feet, his ears out to the sides, now forward,
as he became more sure, but now again unsure, the
ears out sideways again while he snorted. Slocum
watched those ears as he listened to the whispering
leaves, the cries of a bluebird, a meadowlark.

When the horse was more sure of his footing,
Slocum looked up through the tops of the tall, thick
trees, to the high blue sky.

It was when he broke out of the timberline and
looked down a long coulee that he saw the horse
and rider. Instantly he was alert, and taking out the
field glasses he turned them to the figure below,
which, unfortunately, had just ridden around a cutbank. He swung the glasses to the other side of the
cutbank, where the rider would come out. And to
his surprise when the figure reappeared he saw it
was a woman; and, more than that, he saw that the

horse she was riding was about to go lame.

Turning the spotted pony now, he began to quarter down the wide slope of bunch grass toward the cutbank, beyond which a creek probed its way through a line of willows.

He wondered who it could be, this far from town or from any of the cattle spreads. But now, pausing again and looking through the glasses, he recognized not only the face but the figure of Felicia Ziegler. She was already waving at him, though undoubtedly at that distance she couldn't have recognized him.

She was wearing the tightest riding britches he had ever seen. For a moment his eyes were riveted, and he came within an instant of losing himself; recovering as a flash of warning seared him. Riding down from the cabin, at no moment had he lost his attentiveness to the possibility of danger, the chance that the bushwhacker might have cut his trail again. And here, here he had almost thrown himself away. It was in just such moments when the attention fell that a man was lost.

She was riding a dappled grey, and those gorgeous thighs were spread tightly over a brand new stock saddle with silver conchos. Her green silk shirt was open at the throat, pulled tight by her marvelously prominent breasts. A loose white silk scarf hung around her neck, yet neatly, and through an opening he could see the milky contrast of her skin just above the change of contour that began the division of her breasts. Her brown eyes were sparkling with fun as she greeted him, and again he almost lost himself as his passion came to a rolling boil. Still, horny as he was, Slocum hadn't lasted all this while out on the frontier by being indulgent, lazy, or dumb.

"Fancy meeting you way out here, Mr. Slocum. I am delighted, and, I must add, grateful. I'm afraid my horse is going lame."

"So I noticed from up there," he said, nodding toward his backtrail. "How long?" he asked, dismounting.

"A good while. In fact, pretty soon after we left the ranch."

He stared at her straight on as she said that. "Then you should have gone back. You can ruin a horse riding him like that."

But he failed in his effort to shock her. She was unperturbed by his scolding, and even continued to smile, although not with quite as much warmth. "I thought he'd developed a sore muscle, something like that, and would get over it."

"Well, get down and hold his head while I take a look-see. Might be the frog."

"The frog? What on earth's that?" She was standing close beside him now and he could smell her perfume.

"It's part of his hoof," he said. "Now hold him up close to the bridle."

When she took the reins close up as he'd indicated, he turned toward the horse, patting his shoulder, then letting his big hand slide down along the left front leg to the hoof as the animal responded, lifting his foot to the man's touch.

"Got a stone in the shoe." He put the foot down,

reached into his pocket, and brought out his Barlow knife. Then, turning his back to the horse, he reached down again and this time took the fetlock and lifted the foot up between his own legs, so that he was facing away from the animal with the hoof between his own thighs. With the knife he began to pry at the stone that was caught in the loose shoe.

At one point the horse moved and took a small hop with his other foreleg, and Slocum, moving with the other hoof between his legs, adjusted his balance as he spoke softly in the special voice he reserved for his own horses whenever he was working around them. In another moment he had removed the pebble, but the shoe, though loose, was not loose enough for him to pull it off. He released the hoof slowly, stepped away, and stood close to the animal, patting his shoulder. Then he took the reins from the girl and led the horse a few steps.

"Still sore. You'd better not ride him."

"But how am I going to get back home?"

"I reckon I'll have to take you."

When he turned to face her he saw that she had been gazing at him all along, and he found the haughtiness in her eyes, coupled with the curious smile at her full lips, absolutely compelling.

"How marvelously convenient that you happened along!"

He had taken out a quirly and was lighting it.

"Have you another of those?"

"Sure." He liked her forwardness, though he knew it could turn easily into arrogance and aggression.

As he struck the lucifer and lighted the quirly

for her, his eyes caught the gold wedding band on her finger, which she had not been wearing when he met her in town. He wondered who her husband was; perhaps she was Barney Ziegler's daughter-in-law.

He had been wondering about Barney Ziegler lately, too. For he was somehow certain that such a man as he'd heard him described had to be a whole lot more than merely tolerant of the Hamptons and the Ellingers stealing his stock over the years. And he realized suddenly with a bit of a shock that he knew hardly anything at all about Ziegler and the Lazy Z. All the more reason for developing a relationship with Felicia Ziegler, he decided.

They had been standing facing each other, just smoking, but looking, too, and now she spoke, first dropping her eyes and then raising them. "Mr. Slocum, that's very kind of you to offer to see me home. I rode out to have a sort of picnic and brought some sandwiches along. Would you join me? It's a lovely spot here." Her eyes swept the meadow, and then she raised them to look at the sky.

"Sure. If you've got enough. I mean, I don't want to take the food out of your mouth."

She broke into laughter at that. "I even have a bottle of wine. What do you think of that?"

"I think that's great!"

"Something must have told me you'd be along."

And they were laughing together as he helped her take down the blanket roll from her saddle skirt.

He led the short distance to the edge of a copse of alders close to the creek. There they spread the blanket and sat, Slocum making sure he had a clear view of anyone who might approach.

"We'll have to share this," she said, holding up a single cup.

"I don't mind if you don't."

Her laughter tinkled into the bright morning.

It was hot, but not uncomfortable. The sky was totally clear. In the nearby alders a bluebird sang and a group of meadowlarks flickered through the brilliant air, not far above the ground. The dry grass was stretching in the heat, almost crackling, while the water of the creek trilled over its rocky bed. The whole land tingled with sound, each and all of the living things supporting the vast stillness.

The sandwiches were tomato and cheese and she had some baking-powder biscuits and a jar of canned peaches.

"How lucky I brought the extra sandwich," she said.

"Lucky you brought this good wine."

"It is delicious, the wine," she agreed.

Her teeth, he noticed again, were meticulously even and white. Her voice purred in the warm noonday; her eyelids were like velvet as she lowered them a little in contemplation of the cup of wine she was holding. She handed it to him.

She was leaning very slightly toward him as he drank, supporting herself with her left arm, her hand flat on the blanket. A sudden movement of wind blew some of her black hair across her eyes and mouth.

Slocum handed her the cup and as she took it, his eyes felt over the deep curve of her breast pushing so tightly against the green silk blouse that he thought he would surely stretch his trousers out of shape. In fact, that was exactly what was happening, and he made no effort to conceal the fierce drive of his sexual organ. He saw her eyes drop and knew she was looking at it. In the next moment he had taken the cup out of her hand and dropped it in the grass. His arms enveloped her and, like a dance, her mouth received his, and as they fell to the blanket her legs dropped apart, while his hand reached to the inside of those thighs that had been tantalizing him beyond endurance.

Pressing his hand into her crotch as her legs spread farther apart, he felt her wetness coming right through her riding britches. She was already pumping herself against his hand, while her breath came gasping out of her. In another moment he had started unbuttoning her blouse, while she reached down and began pulling off her clothes.

"God, get yours off!" she cried.

Slocum suddenly stood up and, grabbing the blanket, took her hand and began running toward some trees.

"What are you doing?"

"We want some privacy. Hell, you never know who'll come by out here."

"I don't care. I don't care. Here! Put the blanket here!" And when he dropped it she fell down, pulling him with her. "God, Slocum!" And with a great pull she ripped open his fly, plunged her hand inside, and tried to pull his organ out.

"It's too big! I can't get it out!"

"Here, I'll help you."

He drew back his hips so he had a freer move-

ment and with a great tug she yanked his cock out.
It sprang into the air and she squealed with delight,
instantly falling on it with her sucking lips, her
tongue, even her delicious white teeth nibbling at
it. At the same time she was squeezing his balls.
Slocum was on his back and she was over him, on
her knees, and he reached behind her and slid his
thick middle finger up into her wet bush of hair.

When she raised up for air her breasts sprang
into his face, bouncing onto him with nipples that
were long and hard like the end of a finger.

Suddenly he pushed her over on her back and
mounted her, plunging his tremendous shaft all the
way in at one great stroke while she cried out,
begging for it.

They were totally naked now as their bodies
blended into their great passion. Finally they increased their speed, stroking more swiftly and at
the same time more surely as he brought her and
himself to a climax.

They lay locked in each other's arms and legs
now, and Slocum felt the hot sun on his back.

She was fondling his hair. "God, Slocum! What
a man you are! I'd no idea. I knew you had a big
one. I never knew it was *that* big."

"But you made it small," he said.

"I'll make him grow again." And, leaning over,
she bit him lightly on his lip. Then, dropping down,
she began to lick along his thighs, across his belly
and into his belly button, while with the tips of her
fingers she teased along his balls and up along his
member. Bending further, she ran her tongue around
its great dark red head, tickling into its opening

with the tip of her tongue.

At the same time his fingers were exploring her great bush and her soft, soaking lips. And the odor of their sex drove them both to further extremes, as now she rose up and put her bush right over his mouth.

"Kiss it, oh my God, please kiss it!"

He sank his tongue in as far as it would go, then turned her over onto her hands and knees and entered her easily from the rear. Now he rode her around the blanket as she moved forward on elbows and knees. She was almost screaming with joy when he suddenly took it out and she spun on him. "My God, don't do that!"

But he had her on her back and now mounted her with the full length of his thrusting cock and rode her as hard as he had ever ridden anyone, while she responded to every twist and wiggle and push without missing a stroke. They pulsed their way now to a wildness that neither could control. Finally she begged him to come, but he held it, held it for that most exquisite torture until she had really begged all the way—and then they came all the way. And as they came, he looked down at her to see a look of blazing triumph in her wide-open eyes.

It was a distance to the lazy Z. Damp with satiation, Slocum and the girl rode in slowly on the spotted pony, leading the dappled grey. It was at Broken-Back Creek that he knew someone had picked up their trail, falling silent as the girl, straddling the horse behind the cantle of his saddle, first rode with her arms around his waist, her body pressed against

his, and so engendering an increasing desire in him,
and now as he told her to, moving her hands up
simply to touch his shoulders so that he would be
freer with his movement. Her new position did
nothing to slacken his desire. And even as he rode
with all his senses alert, a part of him was still very
much aware of her heat, and the sexual hunger
which seemed at the very core of her being.

His eyes scanned everything within view, but he
could see nothing moving. It was a feeling, really—
the feeling he had known for so many years—his
extra sense.

Then, crossing Broken-Back Creek as it doubled
back for the second time, he saw a movement out
near a wide stand of box elders. But he and the girl
were protected pretty well at the creek, which was
lined with willows and alders and some cottonwoods. He had a feeling it wasn't the bushwhacker,
but rather someone on lookout. Likely an outrider
for the Lazy Z.

Shortly, as they rode within sight of the big ranch
house and the outlying buildings, he got another
glimpse of something moving off to his left. Then
as he drew rein and the girl slipped down from the
spotted pony, he saw the man and horse more clearly.

"Thank you, Slocum," she said, looking up at
him. "I wish you'd change your mind and come on
in for a while."

"I'd like to, but like I said, I've got to get to
town."

"Another time, then?" And she looked up at him,
with her lips parted and her breath moving high in
her bosom. The sunlight glistened in her hair as she

looked down for a moment; then her eyes returned to him.

"Yes," he said, "another time." He was thinking of Big Barney Ziegler, and whoever it was might be her husband, plus the hostility he felt coming now from all around him. At this point he saw three men come out of one of the buildings, which he took to be the bunkhouse.

"Is something the matter?" she asked.

He grinned down at her. "Nothing."

"You looked ... funny for a moment." She was frowning.

"Only thinking how a man's got more privacy smack dab in the middle of San Francisco than in this here place." And with a nod he turned his horse. "So long," he said over his shoulder, and he trotted the pony on out the way they had come. He never looked back, though he could feel her eyes on him, and he kept his right hand close to the Colt at his side.

All the way out of the little valley that held the ranch buildings he felt he was being watched; he was not sure now whether it was one man or a few. He supposed a big man like Barney Ziegler would have enemies and would have enough sense to keep outriders around his place, especially with the Hamptons and the Ellingers fighting each other and the rustling that was going on. He could imagine the feud and its spilling over would be big trouble for a man like Ziegler.

Golightly had told him that Ziegler had been gone from the country for some medical treatment or other in San Francisco and Chicago when the two feisty families had started their fighting, and so wasn't there to handle things at the beginning. Barney had been away a good two years, Doc had told him, and by then the action had a big head start. Since Ziegler's return things had quietened down, the families consolidating what they'd stolen from the Lazy Z and the other outfits, and it was then the falling-out between the Hamptons and the Ellingers had come—just as Slocum himself had figured, over a division of the spoils. And, as he realized now, riding toward The Town, without the easy access to rustling, there was no safety valve for either family to let off steam, and so the boil was on.

He had just come around a cutbank into a little meadow where a herd of eight elk were grazing when he saw the horse and rider coming toward him.

Slocum kept his hand near his gun, but made no overt moves, checking the sides of the trail, and behind the rider for evidence of anyone else, and not slowing his horse's gait. When they were within a few feet of each other the other man drew rein, and Slocum did likewise. He was facing a cowman all right—the way he rode his horse, his chaps, but mostly the trussed bawling calf he was carrying on his horse's withers.

"You—Slocum!"

Slocum took his time answering. And then, squinting at the other man, "Well, it's a gut *you're* not Slocum."

"Mister, I ain't interested in your funnin'. I been following you."

"I know. And don't try getting hard with me, mister. It will not get you anyplace except flat on your ass." Slocum cut those words out like pieces of flint.

The rider was a young man with a hard jaw, which he was clenching as he kicked his horse forward. "Slocum, I am telling you—you stay away from Mrs. Ziegler. You got that?"

"No, I don't got it!" And then, almost overlapping his own words, "But you better stay away from Slocum, mister!"

The other man took a deep breath. His eyes dropped for a moment to the calf, which was struggling to get free while his horse was spooking. He cut his reins fast across the animal's head, then looked straight at Slocum again. Slocum wondered if maybe he was the girl's brother. Certainly he couldn't be her husband. He was sure she wouldn't have picked such a kid. Or maybe he was an in-law. It didn't matter. The young man had kicked his horse closer to the spotted pony, who shied away from the now fully bawling calf, which was working itself loose, though the rider was so angry he clearly was only concerned with Slocum.

Slocum watched his hand inch toward his holster.

His words cracked like a whip. "Leave it right there, son. You'll live longer."

The other's hand froze, and he straightened in the saddle. "Listen, Slocum. You tell those Ellingers or whoever you're with to keep their fucking running iron off of Lazy Z calves." With his middle finger he tapped the animal lying across his pony's withers. "And I am telling you again, stay clear of Mrs. Ziegler. I've heard of you. I know your kind."

"Good, then," said Slocum, and his smile cut across his face like a knife. "Since you know my kind you must know how I answer punk kids who threaten me." And almost before he had finished speaking he had grabbed the other by his shirt collar, yanked him forward and down as he brought his knee up to slam him in the face. Then, with a twist, he pulled him all the way out of his saddle and tumbled him onto the ground. Both horses shied away from the fallen man, while Slocum waited.

Slowly the fallen cowboy pulled himself to his knees. His nose was bleeding and so was his mouth. His eyes were slits as he focused on the man on horseback who had humiliated him. "By God, I don't guess we'll have peace in this country till you goddamn Ellingers and Hamptons all kill yourselves off!"

He was on his feet now, his hands at his sides, his chest heaving as he tried to catch more breath.

"Don't worry about it," Slocum said.

"All right! But get this. My name's Gilhooly. Johnny Gilhooly. I'm the Lazy Z's foreman. Remember that. Remember that name!"

"And you can remember my name, son. It's Slocum. You remember that."

"I'll remember it; I will remember your name, Slocum."

"Good. Because you made the mistake of forgetting it for a minute there."

And Slocum turned his horse to go around Johnny Gilhooly's mount, now kicking him into a brisk canter, leaving the other with great surprise and chagrin spread all over his damp face.

# 6

At first he'd thought they were playing, seeing them
from the top of the rise as he rode in from the north.
The big manure pile was back of the livery barn,
and as Slocum rode closer he discerned that the
four figures were in reality engaged in hard combat.
It was three against one, the single boy being the
smallest. In the fading light it was impossible to
make out any of their features, only that all were
in deadly earnest. The smaller boy seemed to be
putting up a more deadly battle than his attackers.
Suddenly he dropped one of the three, and the other
two, seizing the opportunity of his being off balance, bore in with redoubled fury.

Now the smaller boy was really on the defensive,
for the boy he'd downed rose and charged him, too.
But the boy beat him off with a well-aimed kick in

the groin, and then he smashed another boy in the adam's apple, causing him to stagger around in a circle gasping for air. Meanwhile, curses shredded the early evening air, although as far as Slocum could see no one was sufficiently interested to be a spectator of the gladiators on the manure pile. The Town, of course, had witnessed infinitely more exciting exchanges over the years, and a battle of fisticuffs between young boys was pretty small beer.

But not to the boys. Suddenly the three gave a concerted charge and bore the smaller boy onto his back, where they proceeded to pummel and kick him, shrieking curses and threats. All at once the boy twisted away and was on his feet, throwing clods of manure, then swinging his fists. He was not finished yet, Slocum saw as he drew rein. He had the impulse to interfere, but something stopped him, some unique quality of—dignity, was it?—in the boy as he fought off his attackers, and even at certain points brought the fight to them, not waiting simply to defend himself. And so he waited, not wishing to spoil something, something hard and brutal yet, for all anyone might tell, necessary.

But Slocum could see the boy's arms were slower, his swings almost carrying him off his feet. And suddenly he was down. Gasping curses, he tried in vain to fend off the hail of blows that descended on him. A kick in the stomach doubled him, and he was speedily pounded into unconsciousness.

"That is enough," Slocum snapped. "Leave him be."

They looked up at him now from where they were kneeling on their victim, their breath sawing the air, seeing him for the first time.

"That'll fix the little son of a bitch," one of them said, his face twisted in a sneer, but with the blood running from his nose. He looked down at the inert boy on the manure pile. "Told you yer sister's a goddamn whore, you little bastard!"

"Goddamn fucking whore!" snarled one of his companions as they rose and stood glaring in defiance at the man on the horse.

"Get your asses moving," Slocum said, and there was no nonsense in his words.

They didn't hesitate, but turned and started to run. One of them slid in some wet manure as he started off and fell. He rose quickly and, shrieking after his companions, limped after them, but they had already disappeared around the corner of a building.

Slocum stepped quickly down from his horse and walked up onto the pile of manure to where the defeated battler lay. The small boy was curled with his fists still clenched for battle.

By God, Slocum thought, the kid had surely given an account of himself. The kid had guts to spare. The figure groaned and now, as a light went on in the livery and its ray shafted out onto the man and the boy, Slocum knew who it was. He reached down and turned the boy over, and for a moment he stood there looking down into the cut and bleeding face of Billy Ellinger.

"He'll mend," said Dr. Anse Golightly quickly, pouring milk into the saucer for Thaddeus, who paid no attention to his benefactor, being totally occupied with his refreshment. Doc was referring to his young patient, who had been brought in by John Slocum.

"He's a tough boy," Slocum said, thinking how fortunate it was that the frequently absent Golightly had been in his office at that needed moment.

The boy had been fairly badly beaten but, as Slocum said, he was tough. He sat there saying nothing, except now and again cursing his recent adversaries, while the doctor treated his bruises, abrasions, cuts, wrenches, and twists but, fortunately, no breaks, although the knuckles of his trusty right hand were ominously swollen.

"You're lucky," Doc said as he worked industriously all over Billy's young body. "Lucky I was here, not called out to someone with the croup or whatever." All the time he was working he kept humming a little tune to himself.

Billy had come around quickly, angry, but not for a minute sorry for himself. "I'd of got that big son of a bitch if I hadn't of slid in that horseshit," he said through his swollen lips.

"Who were they?" Slocum asked, though he had an idea. "How did it start?"

"Hamptons." The boy almost spat the word. "It ain't the first time, but it's the first they caught me alone."

"You did right fine," Slocum said.

"I kicked that little Mickey son of a bitch right in the balls, by golly. Excepting I wisht I'd got a crack at that goddamn Burt, the son of a bitch!"

"Burt?" Doc straightened up to look at the boy seated in the chair. "Burt Hampton?"

"It was him started it."

Doc was staring hard at the boy. "You don't mean Burt, Hamp's son?"

"That's who started it, like I said."

Billy looked up at Golightly, then swung his eyes, one of which was almost completely closed, to Slocum.

Slocum let the breath out of his body. "Did he hit you?"

"No. He started it, though. I was walking down there by the livery barn after me and Sis drove in with the gig. Wanted to check that crazy mare. And when I come out, they were there, Burt and the three boys. They're his boys. Sloan, Phil, and Mickey. The four of them was there. And he started in on me."

"Jesus," said Doc Golightly.

"What did he say?" Slocum wanted to know.

"Stuff." The boy dropped his head, and his jaw fell suddenly on his heaving chest. His clothes were torn, his shirt was bloody, mostly from his nose, his yellow hair was everywhere. He was all right now, save for his anger, which was taking a new surge in his battered body.

"Anyways," he went on, his voice lower, edged with pride, "I kicked that little son of a bitch Mickey right where he'll be pissing like a corkscrew for a week, by God!"

"What did Burt do after they started fighting with you?" Slocum asked.

"I dunno. I dunno. They went off somewheres. Then when I'd come out of the barn the three of them was there. Then . . . then I guess you was there."

He raised his head and with his good eye looked at Slocum.

"Jesus," whispered Golightly. "I told you, Slocum, I told you Burt Hampton is a bad 'un. I do believe he's the worst of that Hampton trash." He had started to bandage the boy's hand. "Billy, you get right on home. Where's your sister?"

"She's up to Collender's having coffee. That's where I left her."

"Then you get her and get on home." He nodded his head toward Slocum. "Things are worse, and they're gonna get worser. I knew it. When I heard Burt Hampton was coming back to the Basin I knew. Son of a bitch is worse than his brothers plus Hamp together."

The boy raised his head. "Fuck them!" He said it steadily, as though it were a prayer. And then, realizing something suddenly, he stared at Slocum. "Say, we thought you'd left the country!"

"It looks like I've decided to stay," Slocum said, and he stood back as Doc finished his work and surveyed his patient with a firm look on his face.

"You'll mend," Doc said. "But you be careful from now on. Don't go around without somebody with you. I mean it."

"So why don't you come on back with us?" the boy said, looking at Slocum. "Since you've decided to stay."

Slocum didn't answer. He couldn't help grinning at the suddenly shining blue eyes, the damp stack of yellow hair, and the freckles, a good many of which had been splattered with blood. This time there was no blade of grass.

"Get over there and wash up at that basin," Doc said, and he nodded toward the washstand in a corner of the room. Then, crossing, he poured water from a pitcher and placed a towel for the boy.

"Billy, I want to talk with Slocum, here; you think you can make it all right to Collender's, or shall I get your sister?"

Slocum came in fast then before the boy could react. "'Course he can make it. For crying out loud, Doc, he all but flattened the three of those buggers."

And he watched the grin come painfully into the boy's face. Doc, chastened, grinned ruefully down at Thaddeus, who was now giving him all his attention since the milk was long gone.

"When will you come out, Slocum?" Billy asked, standing up and reaching for his hat.

"Pretty directly. I got some work to do first."

The boy had his big hat on and was pulling his red galluses over his ruined shirt.

Doc eyed the shirt. "Sally's going to appreciate that."

"You run along now, but stay on Main Street," Slocum said. "Tell Sally I'm here if either of you needs me. She will know where I'm staying."

Billy stared in surprise. "She knows?"

"When you tell her I said that, she'll remember a place she told me about."

"Good enough." The grin came again.

Slocum could see he was closer to his old self, or young self—cut lip, plugged-up nose, shiner, bruises, and all. He walked him to the door of Golightly's office while Doc grabbed Thaddeus, who was trying to climb up his pants.

Something in the boy's manner caused Slocum to follow him into the hall.

"Slocum..." The white, earnest face turned up to the tall man. The voice was low, intense, and Slocum could hear his young friend's effort at control.

"Did—did you hear? Did...what they called my sister...?"

"I heard."

"Don't tell her, Slocum." And the blue eyes filled with tears of anger and pain. "Don't tell her...." And, with a choked sob, he hurried down the stairs.

"You be careful, Billy. I'll see you soon." And for a moment he almost went along with him, but he remembered that Billy Ellinger was suddenly not a boy any longer.

When he walked back into the office, Golightly had a drink poured for both of them.

"So you'll be staying a while."

Slocum nodded in appreciation of Golightly's economy of words and thought.

"It's getting dirty," he said.

"Always." Doc lifted his glass. "That young man's a good 'un."

They drank to Billy Ellinger.

"Near as I can reckon," Doc said, "the Hamptons and Ellingers have locked horns—or assholes, if you favor the expression—a dozen times over the past couple of years. Three deaths due to lead poisoning, plus wounded, and in some less dramatic instances, beatings. Howsomever, this is the first time they have stooped to beating up the young. Who's next? The women?"

"It looks to me like they've already started on that."

When Golightly cocked his eye at him, Slocum told him what he had heard at the battle on the manure pile.

Doc shook his head solemnly. He cleared his throat, shaking his wattles some, and then said, "Howsomever, do not get the notion that it's all the Hamptons. The Ellinger crowd is not made up of Sweet Jesuses either. Sam Ellinger, I have heard, pistol-whipped Tom Hampton one fine day right here on Main Street. Tom cashed in shortly after." He sniffed wetly, drank, and, sniffing again, said, "Claimed Thomas looked cross-eyed at his daughter and passed some remark about the same."

"And Barney Ziegler?" Slocum said after a pause. "Where does Barney Ziegler fit in?"

Doc poured from the bottle again and began walking about his office, holding his index finger out like a ruler as he gripped his glass and spoke of the owner of the Lazy Z. "I see Barney about at the end of his patience. He has tolerated these families in the Basin, and the other outfits have gone along with him, figuring if it wasn't the Hamptons and the Ellingers fighting, it'd be something else. The thing is, Barney does not want any more coming into the country. At first, with the Hamptons and Ellingers and the rest of them here, things looked pretty stable. But, as you know, that didn't last. And with Burt Hampton come back to the Basin, it's going to get worse. It's building up to a killing time now. I feel it in my juices." He paused, his bronze eyes wide open on Slocum. "I will allow

that you feel it, too, sir. Ain't that why you're
staying?"

There were too many elements, was the thought
that kept running in his head. Sally and Billy
Ellinger, Cole and the other Ellingers, Burt Hampton, Hamp and the family, Barney Ziegler, the bushwhacker, Harry Poon, and even that uppity kid of
a ranch foreman Gilhooly who'd tried to brace him.
Well, he could understand that. The kid was obviously hot as a pistol for Felicia Ziegler. He wondered about Felicia. He wondered what sort of
husband she had.

These thoughts were running through him as he
rode out to the cabin on Jack Creek. On a hunch,
he had decided to take his own backtrail, the trail
he'd ridden down on his back when the spotted
pony had dragged him. For the thought kept nagging him that the man who had tried to kill him
then might very well be the same one who had been
watching the Ellinger cabin from the timberline
above the meadow. Something just didn't fit, and
Slocum couldn't figure what it was. The only thing
to do in such cases, he knew, was to take action
and see what came together. So the next morning
found him going back over his long drag down the
mountain.

It didn't take as long as he'd thought it would.
And it was satisfying to discover the spot near a
spruce where he had wounded the man. The evidence of flight was still readable in the broken
bushes, in a dropped whiskey bottle, and in the
scattered cartridges. Only he knew for sure it wasn't

Poon. Poon would never have been able to ride through those mountains, not with those lungs and that frail body. And yet, who else could it be? Poon had promised to kill him; sworn it. "Next time," he'd said. "Next time, you are dead, Slocum!" And those fevered eyes had burned like coals. Burning onyx-colored eyes. In Forth Worth when those two cow wranglers had entered the game drunk and one had set down four aces and the other five, and both had reached for the pot. Both were dead now, courtesy of Mr. Poon's swift deliverance. It was Slocum who had objected that such professional action on a couple of young cow waddies was unnecessary and as Poon struck for his big Colt, he found himself already covered by the big man with the raven-black hair and green eyes.

"Two killings is enough, Harry," Slocum had said, as the surprise froze on Harry Poon's thin face.

"Drawed a bit early there, didn't you, Slocum?" the gambler snarled. "You was pulling when you started to talk."

"The thing that counts, Poon, is this gun pointing right at you. It don't matter a damn how it got there. You make one move and I'll cut you in two."

Slowly the gambler lowered his Colt, the smoke from his shooting the two card players still hanging over the green baize-topped table.

"You win this time, Slocum. I will win the next round." Those black eyes looked like two bullets at Slocum. Then something had seemed to relax inside him. "I am not looking for suicide this day," he said. And in a fresh, reflective tone, "He dies twice who perishes by his own hand." A cold smile suddenly appeared under the thin mustache. "Publius Syrus." And he added, "The source of my quotation."

Poon must know that he was here in Sunshine Basin. Cole Ellinger had said the name, said Poon had been hired by Hamp Hampton. He had never thought of Poon as a hired gun. Poon was famous as a gambler, and mostly a gunfighter, but not a man for hire. Perhaps that was only a cover for his closing in on the man who had humiliated him. But what about the man who had followed him? Where was he?

Still puzzled, Slocum started back to Jack Creek. Well, the only thing to do was to keep moving, he decided. And by the time he reached the cabin, he had his plan ready. By the time he reached the cabin he had already figured out what he needed to know about the bushwhacker, and about Harry Poon. The picture was really not as complicated as it had appeared. It was all quite simple. For he knew now that the bushwhacker had never intended to kill him.

When he rode into the little meadow near Jack Creek he had the feeling that there was company. And sure enough, there was the dun horse with the three white stockings in the corral next to the cabin.

As he stepped down from his horse and led him into the corral, she came out of the trees where she had evidently been waiting for him.

"Slocum . . ." And suddenly she was running toward him; in a moment she was wrapped in his arms, her face buried against his chest.

"Thank God you came! I've been waiting."

"What's the matter? Is Billy all right?"

"Billy's all right. It's not him. I've got to talk to you. I hope it's all right I came."

"I told you to, didn't I? Any time." He put his arm around her shoulders.

She said, "Cole and the whole family are getting ready for a big fight with the Hamptons."

"I'm not surprised, after what happened to Billy."

"It's even more than that." She was still somewhat out of breath as she looked desperately at him, but managing all the same to control herself. "It's the cattle drive. The Hamptons really are planning to drive right through our place. Cole has always held out against gunfighting, even not wanting to fight the drive. But this thing with Billy fired him off."

"Don't you think that's what the Hamptons want?"

Tears welled in her eyes. "Oh, my God, it's just too horrible! Why are they all this way? Why can't they be decent? Killing one another isn't going to solve anything. Why do they act this way?"

He watched tears fill her eyes.

"It's . . . horrible," she said.

"What's the actual situation right now? Do you know? Are they going to carry the fight to the Hamptons, or wait for the drive to start?"

"I don't know. All I know is that Uncle Cole sent Carl Wiley to tell us to get out, that there was going to be a big fight, and we'd better get out or we'd be in the middle of it." She paused, regaining the breath she had expended in her emotion. "But I had already heard how angry Cole was about Billy.

He is . . . well, he's blaming the whole thing on Burt Hampton."

"Maybe you and Billy better move up here," Slocum said. He was facing her, looking down into her face, and when she lowered her eyes, looking at the sunlight dancing on the top of her dark hair. When she lifted her eyes her tears had dried, and she had changed into a firm young woman of action.

"I wish there was something . . . something we could do. Isn't there something, Slocum? You know, if Cole fights Burt Hampton it will start up a whole thing. Even without the cattle coming through. But all the men want to fight."

"That's understandable; they've been diddling with it for too long. Something was bound to explode. And this is it. If it hadn't been Billy, it would have been something else," he said, his voice soft.

They had started walking toward the cabin.

"I've got to get back to Billy. Maybe we will come up here."

"I think that's the best thing to do." He stopped and, raising his head, watched an eagle sweeping down the long blue sky. "I want to know something," he went on.

"What is it?"

"Just where does Barney Ziegler's range end and the Basin range begin?"

"I don't know exactly, but it's around Crazy Man Creek; all that country north is his, I believe, and this side of the creek is Hampton and Ellinger. Most of the Basin." She looked up at him with a puzzled expression on her face. "Why do you ask?"

"Just wondered. I've got another question. Who

is to the west of the Basin?"

"Do you mean on the other side of the big ridge?"

He nodded. "I heard that was sheep country."

"Manacle Ridge is the dividing line between sheep and cattle country; at least, that's how I've always understood it. Some years ago, before any of the Ellingers or Hamptons were here, Barney Ziegler made a truce with the sheepmen, agreeing that the Ridge would be the line between cattle and sheep. They were on the point of a war then, too, I've heard."

"Who are the sheepmen?"

"Mostly Clarence Herkimer." She stared hard at him. "Slocum, what are you getting at?"

"I'm not sure myself. I was just studying all the angles here. There has got to be a way out; otherwise, you're going to have the whole Basin throwing lead and killing each other off." And suddenly he stopped.

"What is it?"

"I dunno. I was trying to remember something Johnny Gilhooly said the time I ran into him."

"I'd better get back to Billy," she said after a moment when he didn't continue.

"Where is Cole now?" Slocum asked.

"I don't know. Probably at his place."

But she saw he wasn't listening to her, as he stood squinting at the sky.

"Slocum . . ."

"Get inside the cabin. Quick! And bolt the door."

And, reaching up to the rifle scabbard on his still saddled horse, he drew the Winchester.

She was already running to the cabin, and in a

moment he had disappeared into the timber, and only just in time before the three horsemen appeared. He had been wondering if possibly it was Cole and some of the Ellingers with him still trying to enlist his help. But to his surprise it was neither Ellinger nor Hampton. It was Johnny Gilhooly, accompanied by two men he had never seen before.

They rode right up to the corral, not trying to cover their presence at all.

"Hold it right there!"

The three drew rein, their hands dropping free so that Slocum could see they were nowhere near their guns.

"What do you want, Gilhooly?"

"Mr. Ziegler wants to talk to you." The foreman turned toward the direction of the voice, but could see no one.

Slocum changed his position before speaking again in case there might be a fourth horseman to the rear, lining him up for a shot.

"You tell Ziegler it's just as far from me to him as it is from him to me. And he can ride on over any time."

"Maybe you ain't been told, Slocum," Gilhooly said, speaking slowly and making no effort to disguise the venon in his words, "but Mr. Ziegler can't ride a horse. He can't even walk."

The day was piling surprise on top of surprise, Slocum decided. "And it takes three men to deliver this invite?" He was again changing his position; listening, always. Listening to the country, listening in between the sentences. But there was nothing out of the ordinary. He watched the ears on the three horses for any indication of another horse nearby, but there was nothing.

"Barney was saying that you could ride back with us. The boys here just come along with me to check some of the Lazy Z stock."

"You tell him I'll come see him."

"Slocum..."

"Git!"

He watched it cutting into Gilhooly's face, which was still showing signs of its encounter with Slocum's knee.

Then, without another word, spitting furiously over his horse's withers, Johnny Gilhooly turned the animal and, followed by his two companions, rode back the way they had come.

Slocum waited until he was sure. Then he came out of the trees and slipped the Winchester into the saddle scabbard on the spotted pony. Then he walked to the cabin.

"What do you think Ziegler wants?" Sally asked as she let him in.

"I dunno. Maybe he's thinking of offering me a job. Some people think I'm a gun for hire."

"Maybe he's heard something of this latest trouble and he's concerned. He always has been concerned that there be peace in the Basin."

"That's nice," Slocum said, and she looked at him suddenly, catching his sardonic tone.

Noticing her expression and not wanting to answer the question he saw coming, he said, "Ziegler must be one of those mind-teller people."

"How do you mean?"

"I mean wanting me to come see him when that was just what I was aiming to do anyway."

It was something that Johnny Gilhooly had said, out by the butte when they'd confronted each other. And seeing the Lazy Z foreman again had brought the words right to the front of his mind. "By God!" Gilhooly had said, "I don't guess we'll have peace in this country till you goddamn Ellingers and Hamptons all kill yourselves off!"

It was this that had been nagging in his mind, and seeing the foreman just now at the cabin had brought it to some kind of point.

Now, riding out to the Lazy Z, past Manacle Ridge, he decided to take a look around. The ridge was a formidable block of land, making a more than adequate land divider for the sheep and cattle to keep separated. Slocum tried to imagine what sort of man Barney Ziegler might be, a man who it seemed was on the order of the toughest cattle barons, a man who had fought and won a sensible arrangement with the sheepmen, and at the same time had kept the cattle ranchers from wiping out the herders. Doc Golightly had given him some of the details, emphasizing how Barney Ziegler was and always had been adamant about clean grazing for cattle.

But his thoughts began to turn toward Felicia Ziegler and he wondered if he would see her when he visited her father-in-law.

Riding up from Eagle Creek past the twin cutbanks and in full view of the Lazy Z buildings, he knew he was being watched.

The noon sun was hot, and he could feel it on his back, and when he leaned forward, on the back of his neck. He was smoking a quirly, and finding he had just a trace of stiffness, not having completely broken in from his layoff at the Double E.

His eye caught a rider off to his left just slipping down a draw, while to his right another was briefly outlined. When he reached the box elders and dropped from sight of the log ranch houses he felt more at ease, although he knew he was still attended. It was a strange moment to lose his tension like that, but he had no time to concern himself. Lifting the gait of his horse now he rode up a shallow draw and came suddenly right onto the Lazy Z bunkhouse.

Slocum kept his eyes straight ahead, watching with side vision as half a dozen men came out of the bunkhouse and stood facing in his direction, their hands close to their weaponed hips.

He didn't hesitate, turning his horse now and riding right up the six men, and drawing rein.

"What do you want?" one of them asked, surly.

"Where is Gilhooly?" Slocum said, his tone no less unfriendly than that of the man who had spoken.

But before the man could answer, Slocum saw the foreman come out of the bunkhouse. "I am right here, Slocum."

"Good enough. Tell your boss I am here to see him."

He watched the color hit the young foreman's face and for a moment half expected him to make a play, but Gilhooly thought better of it. "Follow me," he said after a beat. "Mr. Ziegler is expecting you."

Somehow he hadn't expected her that abruptly. The door opened and there she was, her hand on the latch, wrapping him in her sparkle and obvious delight at seeing him.

"Fancy! Mr. Slocum, I do believe. What a pleasure!" And then, not even looking at Gilhooly, she said, "Thank you, Johnny." And Slocum could feel the man beside him stiff as a bullet. He was at once wishing that they were anywhere but in her father-in-law's house, and determined now to make a time when they could meet. And yet, at the same time, not for an instant did he lower his guard.

She had taken his hand and now let it go slowly, turning to lead him into another room. Like the whole house, the room was built of logs which had been peeled and oiled. There were bright-colored rugs on the pine floor, while all the furniture except an old rocking chair, a horsehair sofa, and a rolltop desk had been built of wood and animal hide.

It was another surprise to find the owner of the Lazy Z actually in a wheelchair, though Gilhooly had told him Ziegler couldn't walk or ride. Yet Slocum was in for a bigger shock as the girl turned toward him again, saying, "Mr. Slocum, I'd like to introduce you to Barney Ziegler." And then she added, "My husband."

Barney Ziegler was from the Panhandle and it might have been he who, when looking over the great plains of Wyoming, first minted the phrase, "I never

been in this part of Texas before." But then, it might
not. No matter; he was highly capable of such an
observation. Barney Ziegler thought big, and he
was big; sitting like a buffalo with that massive
steel-grey head and those bull shoulders in that
wheelchair that seemed more part of him than not,
such was the man's force.

That little buckskin bronc had only made him
more Barney Ziegler than before. The one that had
stomped him. Thrown him, and stomped him! Stove
him up!

Barney at sixty was as tough and ornery as ever;
more so. But he was a loner, save for his women.
His sons had left, not able to compete with the man
who, even when stove and in that chair being carried all over the ranch, still ran everything with a
hand of iron, sometimes in a cactus glove.

He could stand now, but not for very long. And
he was pretty straight up and down, for he wore a
brace made especially for him in San Francisco by
a leather-worker of top quality. At night, alone, he
removed the brace. But nobody was around then,
except whatever woman was his at the moment.
And the woman, it was said, would inevitably mar-
vel, for, paralyzed or not, his masculinity was all
it should be. At least this was the gossip and rumor,
the legend, nurtured by Barney himself. Only those
immediately involved, of course, could know what
was truth and what was not. In any event, legend
or no, all agreed that Barney Ziegler was no man
to mess with.

"I have heard of you, Mr. Slocum." The hand
he offered was big, a paw, and hairy; the grip gentle

with power. Slocum could feel that power, and he gave it back.

"I have heard of you, Mr. Ziegler. What can I do for you?"

Barney Ziegler inclined his head toward a chair. "My wife will bring us something to drink, and we can talk. And I have some fine Havanas in that silver box there. Help yourself."

Slocum didn't have to lift the box; Felicia was already there holding it open. Of a sudden he caught Ziegler's baleful glare. It was a look that explained the whole man to him in a flash—the jealousy, the drive for power, the brutality which was so manifest in the apparent gentleness in his handshake.

"I'll take one," he said.

And once again, Slocum noted the revealing gesture as Ziegler, his eyes on his visitor, reached to the proffered silver box without even an acknowledgement of his wife. Nor did Felicia Ziegler appear to mind the rudeness and contempt. For plainly, she was no sweet little flower herself; to this Slocum could attest, and their passion scene sprang full blown into his mind and, he noted, with a quick covering movement of his legs, into his trousers. He was pleased to see that the movement had not escaped her, revealing her feelings in the smile at the corner of her mouth.

"Now then." Barney Ziegler's words fell like the title of a legal document into the fresh cigar smoke that plumed into the room as they lighted up.

The door clicked shut behind Felicia as Slocum marveled at her cool handling of her husband.

Ziegler must have been at the very least thirty years older than his wife, and yet it seemed in a certain way to Slocum that it was she who was senior. It amused him to once again realize that so much, if not all, of life's dramas and relationships had their genesis in the bedroom. It was in bed that wars were won and lost—and cattle kingdoms. Of this he had not the slightest doubt.

"I'll get to the point, Slocum." Barney Ziegler had taken the cigar out of his mouth and was looking at the lighted end of it. He began to speak now as though addressing the ash forming there.

"I was the man who opened this country here. Maybe you know that. No matter. It is still interesting to know who did what in our nation's history. I fought the Crows, the Shoshones, just as down in the Panhandle I fought the Kiowa and the Comanches. A lot of those redskins ain't here any longer. I am." His eyes flicked dead on to his visitor—dark, luminous eyes that reminded Slocum suddenly of a grizzly he'd once tangled with.

"And I fought the outlaws, the rustlers and owlhooters, and rival cattlemen. I am now in the throes of suffering the presence of a bunch of goddamn fools who are bent on exterminating each other and ruining this country. I refer to the Ellingers and Hamptons who are only here courtesy of myself who gave them a helping hand some years back— only to have that hand bitten by the sons of bitches."

Barney Ziegler paused. "I had said I would get to the point, and I haven't. But here it is." Suddenly he was overcome by a fit of coughing. He shook,

hacking and bringing up phlegm, spitting into the
cuspidor beside the wheelchair, his face flaming
red with the effort.

Suddenly the door burst open and Felicia swept
in, a glass of water in her hand. It was evident that
the attacks were not uncommon, for she seemed to
know exactly what to do, holding the glass for
Ziegler to drink, and then asking if he wanted more
water.

Ziegler was wheezing, but now more under control as his breath returned. "No . . . no!" he snapped.

Without a word, without a glance at Slocum, she
left the room.

A silence fell upon them.

"Where was I? The point . . . yes, that's it. The
town needs a marshal. How about it? We need a
lawman real bad." He held up his hand to forestall
anything in the way of an objection. "It'll come to
more than marshal's pay, Slocum. The point is, I
will pay you whatever you want."

"The point is," Slocum said, feeling his ire rising, "what it is you want."

"I believe I just told you." The thick grey eyebrows leveled at him like the horns on a Brahma
steer, Slocum thought, and he wanted to laugh.

You mean you want me to do whatever you want
me to do. The answer is no."

"I want you to settle this goddamn fighting in
the Basin, Slocum. I've thought of hiring more
guns. I've got plenty right now. And, sure, we can
pump enough lead into the Hamptons and Ellingers
to keep them underground from now on. But what
good is that? They'll be bound to shoot up some

of the Lazy Z, and I ain't about to start shooting myself. With a man like you behind that tin star we'll have a peaceful community for a change."

He paused, while Slocum studied him. He knew that like most big men in the West Ziegler didn't carry a gun. There was no need to when you were that size. Any damn fool throwing down on a Ziegler would be too well known overnight, and wouldn't have a place to hide. None of the really big cattle-men packed a weapon.

But Slocum was wondering just how many guns Ziegler did have. First of all, he didn't believe his big brag about guns at his disposal. Sure, he must have some, but any big outfit with heavy armaments wasn't going to have some young kid like Johnny Gilhooly as ramrod. Gilhooly was just a mite older than being a milky kid, and Slocum doubted he had what it took to kill a man in cold blood.

He had been looking at the elk head on the far wall, and now he felt Ziegler's eyes on him.

"How about it? I have heard of you. Like I say, you can name your price."

"I'm on my way to California."

The big eyebrows shot up. "I don't believe that."

"Don't, then."

For a moment they sat there looking at each other. "What can I offer you to take the job?" Ziegler asked.

"Nothing. I would have thought you had more sense. Can't you tell when a man isn't for sale?"

"Every man has his price, Slocum. Every man. It might not be money." He paused; with his elbows on the arms of the wheelchair he arched his fingers together in front of his big chin. "Sometimes it's land. Sometimes it's women." He reached for his cigar. "Don't be hasty. Think it over."

She was standing outside the room when he came out. "Does he want anything?" Her eyes quizzed him as she looked up, holding her hands behind her back in a semi-playful manner.

"He didn't say."

"Then we'll let sleeping dogs lie. He'll be taking a nap now, and Denvers will get him anything he wants." And she added, "Denvers is the cook."

He was looking down at her, as neither of them moved toward the front door. She still held her hands behind her back, and began a gentle swinging from side to side.

"That's my room over there," she said, nodding to a door to his left.

"Handy."

"Want to take a look? There's a wonderful view."

"What of?"

"The ceiling, of course."

He had started to follow her across the hall. "It's next to your husband's room there," he said.

She had stopped with her hand on the knob of her bedroom door and was facing him. "He won't hear us."

She had dropped her eyes to the bulge in his trousers, which were stretched as far as they could go. Slocum didn't think he could stand any more. Finally she turned and opened the door, and he followed her inside.

He watched her close the door and lock it, and in the next instant she was in his arms, with her leg wrapped around him as she pushed herself up against his rigid member.

"Oh, my God, Slocum. Take my clothes off. Undress me!" He started to pull her toward the bed.

"Undress me first. Please!"

"I'm going to, don't worry."

"But now. Please! First!"

And she took his hand and slipped it inside the neck of her dress, as she rubbed herself against his plunging organ.

Something in her voice caught him, and it was then that he heard a sound that seemed to come from the wall behind her.

"What's that?"

"I don't know. I don't know!" And she had closed his mouth with hers as she began pulling off his clothes and her own.

And then suddenly something clicked. He grabbed her by the shoulders, spun her, and threw her onto the bed.

"Oh, my God, yes!" she cried.

"Oh, my God, no—you goddamn bitch!"

Slocum stood by the bed, pulling in his shirt and buttoning his trousers while the girl sat up on the bed, her breasts springing into the room as her blouse fell down.

"What the hell . . . !"

"You tell that son of a bitch next door if he can't do it himself, I am not going to do it for him and his peephole." And as he said it, more of it came

into line and he added, "The two of you go back
to doing it with Gilhooly. I don't guess he minds
Ziegler watching him.

He didn't bother closing the door as he left the
room. He had already loosened the leather thong
on the Colt, but nobody was there to try to stop
him. In a few minutes he was on the spotted pony
riding fast toward Jack Creek.

Johnny Gilhooly watched him leave. He was standing by the barn, and he felt pretty good about it.
He didn't figure on Slocum coming back. When he
walked up to the main house, Felicia called him
into his employer's room.

There was a strange sort of grin on Barney
Ziegler's face as he said, "I want you to get hold
of Herkimer."

The ranch foreman's face opened in huge surprise. "Herkimer? Clarence Herkimer?"

"Who the hell do you think I am meaning? I
want him here no later than tomorrow morning."
He glared at Felicia, who had followed Gilhooly
into the room.

"You can go," he said, snapping his eyes at Gilhooly. "And remember! Not a word to anyone!"

When he was gone, Felicia said, "Herkimer?
What do you want with Herkimer?"

"You mean what do I want with sheep? Isn't that
what you're asking?"

She nodded.

"I've told you. Did you think I was fooling?"

"I wasn't sure."

"You had better start believing it, then. I am near

broke. I need that range that the Ellingers and Hamptons are using. Right?"

"I understand you this far. But I cannot understand a cattleman wanting anything to do with sheep. Maybe I'm not seeing something. And why did you offer Slocum a job?"

"To get him out of the way. He's dangerous where he is. As for Clarence Herkimer, I am taking him up on an offer he made me some time ago."

"But, as I understand it, cattle won't feed on land where sheep have been."

"That is so. That is one of the reasons for cattle and sheep wars."

"Then—you want to run sheep on your land! I don't understand."

"Correction. Not on this range here. On the Ten Fork. Right next to the Basin. This clever maneuver will not only bring in money, but will throw panic into the cattlemen. Panic! The Hamptons will swear the Ellingers are behind it, and the Ellingers will swear it's Hamp Hampton!"

He was grinning at her, his eyes fondling her big breasts. "Why is it so hard for you to get my point? Don't you know there's more than one way to skin a cat? I knew Slocum would turn me down, but now it's on record I tried to get the law into this thing."

"You mean? You mean you're going to help Herkimer take Sunshine Basin from the Ellingers and Hamptons."

"I'm going to help myself get the Basin. I'm going to finally get those sons of bitches to wipe themselves out, and I'll take over the whole shebang." He lifted his cigar, his dark eyes looking ahead. "Maybe I'll even get rid of old Herkimer."

"So you've been fanning this feud all along," she said, nodding her head as it came together.

"Let's say I haven't been hindering things. I have made good use of what was there already." His face took on a new color and his voice rose. "Why do you think they've been fighting all this time? Who do you think encouraged that Donnybrook and kept them at it? Who but kind, thoughtful, soft-hearted Barney, who is only doing it for his sweet little itsy-bitsy fluff! You're expensive, you know."

"But you like me that way."

"You know what way I like you."

She was standing before him, her cheeks coloring, as he began feeling himself between his legs.

"Let me do that," she said.

"Take your top off. Just the top."

In a moment she had removed her blouse and dropped her chemise so that her breasts were exposed. Kneeling down, she began to stroke him with one hand while with the other she unbuttoned his trousers.

"I'd better lock the door," she said, without stopping, and not looking up.

"Leave it unlocked," he said. "Somebody might walk in."

# 7

As he rode away from the Lazy Z, Slocum was thinking again how it took all kinds to make the mare go, Felicia Ziegler being the latest. His view of Barney Ziegler had taken on a new interpretation. What was he up to? Slocum had the feeling that the Lazy Z was in trouble. And yet there was nothing really definite for him to go on—only the feel of the place. It had the feel of being rundown. And Ziegler had the feel of a power driver, a man who had to be on top at all costs. Yes, that was it. There was the smell of desperation around Barney Ziegler. And the extent of his interesting sexual pursuits only proved that the man was extremely insecure. Was it from his accident with the bronc, or something else, Slocum wondered. Had he always been a Peeping Tom?

It didn't matter. Slocum didn't care, never had cared what people did or thought about sex. He had all he could handle for himself. And at that moment, while by no means writing off Felicia Ziegler, his passion for Sally Ellinger was stronger than ever.

And yet ... And yet, he saw he was still not riding away. Something, not only his physical desire, was holding him here in Sunshine Basin. His thoughts suddenly turned to Poon and the man who had shot him on the mountain trail. What had he been up to? Why had he not tried to kill him? And where was Poon? Still with the Hamptons? Had they really hired a bunch of gunmen? Or just Poon? Poon, to be sure, was worth three of anyone else. But Slocum marveled at the man's pride, if that was the word. For to have followed him, or had Slocum followed all the way from Texas, was no small thing. Or had he just happened to turn up in Sunshine Basin? Ellinger had said the Hamptons had hired him all the way from Forth Worth. Well, they must be desperate, or so caught in their fury they could see nothing else. And the Ellingers? Cole would fight now, that was sure. They'd simply kill each other off. And, as Sally had asked, who would benefit from that?

Slocum kicked his horse into a faster gait. The answer to that was as clear as the daylight around him. The only thing he wondered was how Barney Ziegler would pull it off. Had he plotted the whole feud from the beginning? He had been away when it started. Probably not. Yet he surely had taken advantage of the elements, more than likely adding to the fire with gossip, rumor, and now and again overt action from Johnny Gilhooly and maybe others.

And Ziegler had tried to get him, Slocum, on
his side, using Felicia for bait. He had to hand it
to him, all right. Ziegler played every card in the
deck, and even a few extras.

Maybe there was still time. Maybe . . . And, for
a moment, he asked himself what he was doing.
Why mess with it? It wasn't his business. He could
ride on, letting Poon catch up with him—Poon and
the bushwhacker—at some other time and place.
The West was big in time and place. A man had
always the rest of his life. And sure, the time for
that might be short, the time it takes for getting off
a shot or for the noose to snap your neck if you
were lucky enough to get a good drop. And the
space? Six by six was all a man needed. He could
ride on.

But Slocum knew he wasn't going to. He knew
that something in him had already decided. There
wasn't a thing he could do, he knew. There was
nothing he could do about the Ellingers or Sunshine
Basin. But when he thought of Billy Ellinger, he
knew there was nothing he could do but make a
stab at it.

Clarence Herkimer was a man reaching into his
eighties. He had long since forgotten his age. A
brisk-tempered man with a knobby body encased
in leather. Looking at him, some people were reminded of a shillelagh. Others just saw him as a
tough old geezer who could bite a nail in two without too much effort. It was Herkimer who had first
brought the sheep into the country; Herkimer, and
some Basque herders. They, too, had fought the

Indians and the cattlemen. Herkimer had traded bullets with Barney Ziegler in the old days. Each knew the other's strengths and, just as important, his weaknesses. The two adversaries were just as untrusting, as unforgiving as ever.

"What can I do for you, Barney?"

Clarence sat on the edge of his chair, unaccustomed as he was to the indoor life. For, even though a man of decent means, he seldom lived anywhere except in the great outdoors. He had a potato-shaped nose and, tilting back his head as he surveyed his surroundings, he gave the impression to his host that he was looking down that organ at what he saw. Barney didn't mind. Barney knew, and Clarence Herkimer also knew, that the only reason they were meeting was because Barney Ziegler had a use for his old adversary; and if Clarence Herkimer could find a use for Barney Ziegler then they would do business.

"You mentioned a while back as how you'd like to move some of your woolies into the range just north of Ten Fork."

"Did I?"

Barney ignored the sidestep and continued. "And you said you'd be grateful—financially—if an arrangement could be worked out."

"Exceptin', Mr. Barney Smart Ziegler, you told me I was pissing into the wind, that by God you wasn't leasin' any cattle range to a bunch of filthy, fucking woolies what'd crop out the roots of the graze and shit and piss all over it!" And Herkimer's eyes seemed to bulge out of his head, which appeared to be throbbing under all that exertion. "I mind the time, by God! I mind it!"

"That was some while back, Clarence," Barney countered smoothly, noting how the other hadn't changed a bit, still ornery as a rattlesnake with a thorn up his ass. But Barney had learned how to deal with the old man.

"Well, I finally let some of your hoss sense slip into me, Clarence," he continued. "I have finally seen that you had a good idea there. I have got some use for that range, I won't say I don't need it; but I want good neighbors, and you and me, we have been neighbors since the old days, since long before any of these here new folk came into the Basin and environs."

"Not hoss sense, Barney. Sheep sense."

But Barney saw that he had scored, and he reached to the rolltop desk and brought out a bottle and two glasses.

"Don't mind if I do, by golly," said Clarence, licking his dry lips as Barney poured. "Ain't had a drop since I last visited The Town."

Barney let the bottle pause for a moment as he cocked an eye at his guest, and a sly grin crept into his face. "Hah? At Sister Ellie's place, I'll wager. Eh, you old dog!"

Together they began to chuckle as they knocked their glasses together.

"Well, I did have me a good go-round at Sister's," Clarence allowed, softening liberally under the stroke of Barney's good whiskey. It was not trade stuff, by golly, the sheepman noted. It was prime.

"Man needs it every now and again," Barney admitted, running the tip of his tongue along his lips, enjoying not only the taste but the smell of that good amber fluid.

"Now more than again," put in Clarence with emphasis, his milky eyes clearing suddenly, the unusual expression taking his host by surprise.

But Barney Ziegler took hold of himself, warning himself not to get carried away. Trouble was, he kind of liked the old coot there; he admired that he was the last of a breed, like himself, by damn.

"Clarence, you and me are the last of a breed," he said, the whiskey streaming through his body.

"Maybe. Maybe last of a breed, whatever the hell that is," said the old man. "But right now I'm in the mind to be first down at Ellie's. By damn, I ain't had it since the last time."

"Good enough," Barney said, his big face folded in geniality, "but now we better get down to business."

Some kind of rumbling and rattling seemed to be coming from the old man in the chair opposite him, and Ziegler realized that he was laughing.

"I do agree, Barney. I mean I agree, we could get down to business. Business comes first; and that's a gut. I do agree."

But Barney Ziegler could see that the old man's attention was really elsewhere. Indeed, it was exactly where he wanted it to be—in his pants. "Clarence, I've got my gig and a spanky new mare who can pace the best of 'em. It isn't all that far into The Town. How about joining me for some fun?"

The surprise in Herkimer's face almost made Barney laugh. "You think this here stops a man like

me, Clarence?" And he banged his hand on the arm
of his chair.

"No offense, Barney."

"None taken. And I do take it that you're accepting my invitation. The party's on me." Reaching into the papers on his desk, he found the bell
he was looking for and began ringing it.

When Felicia came into the room, he said, "Mr.
Herkimer and I are going to town. Will you tell
Gilhooly to get the gig ready, and the bay mare.
Tell him to hurry." As he said this last, he kept his
eyes on Clarence Herkimer's face.

"A lot of things can happen to a man in this life,
Clarence. Like this good thing that's happening to
you. I mean Ten Fork."

"I ain't made up my mind yet, Barney."

"You've got nothing to lose, Clarence."

"Barney, you sure you can handle Sister Ellie's?"

For a moment, Barney Ziegler almost made the
mistake of letting the anger hit him. But he remembered what a shrewd bargain Clarence Herkimer
could drive. The old codger was tough all right;
and now he was trying to knock him off balance.
The son of a bitch! Not even the liquor or women
could pull his hand out of his purse. By God, he
mustn't forget that. But Sister Ellie and her girls
were going to help. He'd see to that.

Barney's smile was all over his face as he looked
at his guest. "Clarence, in answer to your question:
it goes like this. Sure, a man can lose the use of
his two legs; like for a while anyway, or maybe
forever. But don't forget, a real man's always got
his third leg."

They were roaring and gasping with laughter, whipping their arms through the air, and almost collapsing with it all when Felicia came in and told them the gig was ready.

Harry Poon had done something that he had never done before. For about the time it took to carefully light a good Havana, or open a bottle of good wine, he had reflected on how times had changed, and with the times, of course, the values. How unlike himself it was to hire someone to track an adversary—in this instance, John Slocum, with whom he'd had the altercation at cards down in Fort Worth at Jicarilla Bob's Good Times Saloon and Gaming Establishment.

But Harry hadn't spent all the time and effort at practicing his trade at cards, dice, and gambling in general, not to mention gunfighting, to allow without passing such a besmirching of his stock in trade as Slocum had brought about. The situation wasn't good for business, in the first place; and, even more, it wasn't good for Harry Poon.

"Egotism," he had often quoted, "is an alphabet of one letter." To which he would more often than not add another quotation: "An egotist is especially hated by all other egotists."

In short, Harry Poon's reputation was at stake; even the suggestion that someone even *might* have backwatered him was not acceptable.

Hammerhead Hogan, the former Wells, Fargo guard, had been looking for work. Having been fired from the express company for various petty, and to be sure dishonest reasons, he seemed to be

the man for the spot. Harry had explained to
Hammerhead carefully—it was not for nothing that
Algernon Hogan had been named Hammerhead by
his associates—that he wanted a man tracked, shot
at but not rubbed out, but followed so that he would
be in a place where he, Poon, could reach him when
he was ready. For, plainly, Harry himself couldn't
cut Slocum's trail. He was definitely not a man of
the trail. He was seldom seen on a horse, though
he rode the girls as often as they and his own so-
briety would let him. Hammerhead, withal, had
done a good job. Slocum had been shaken, wounded,
slowed down, and very likely was puzzling over it
all. In a word, he was in a state where Harry, who
fully realized his powers at arms were not what
they once were, could deal.

Unfortunately, at the moment Harry would have
liked to force the issue with Slocum, his health—
never good even at its best, for he'd been shot
through a lung and had developed consumption—
took a turn for the worse. Still, fortune had changed
her frown into a smile. At the moment Harry received news that Hammerhead had located his
quarry, thanks to meeting up with the posse that
Slocum was eluding, a letter came from Wyoming
suggesting that Harry might be interested in "helping out" at Hamp Hampton's Double H outfit up
near the Greybull Valley. It had all dovetailed. Harry,
a poet at heart, and in the mind, too, fully appreciated how Fortune had worked in his favor. "Fortune aids the bold," as the Spanish saying had it.

He had come to decent terms with Hamp
Hampton, being in charge of a cadre of gunmen

which included Hamp's three sons. Each morning, and sometimes again in the afternoons, Harry conducted lessons in the art of drawing and shooting with a handgun, rifle shooting, plus the various uses of the sawed-off shotgun and the bellygun. He was marvelously adept at all these weapons, and his pupils gave him their best attention.

"The important thing to remember in this activity," Harry Poon would tell his pupils in his sonorous voice, which was every now and again laced with a soft whistle as though he was leaking air somewhere—which he probably was—"is to remember that there is only one winner in a gunfight, or occasionally none."

He would pause, wiping vigorously at his long nose and spitting a little into his handkerchief, then looking at the contents. Everyone of course knew he was a lunger, but no one knew what went on in his mind at such moments.

"Be it known amongst you that animal cunning will kill more men than all other violent causes combined, including snakebite." Pause. "A shot in the back is the most effective means of dispatching an unwanted person, especially when delivered at short range; it requires no great intelligence to pull the trigger and it is relatively safe." He would then let his baleful eyes move slowly around the assemblage.

They were for the most part amused at his droll conversation, but few heard him. What they all liked were the demonstrations, and sometimes even the stories of certain passages-at-arms. Harry showed them how to draw fast for surprise, or slow for better accuracy, how to bluff a man, how to buffalo someone with a gun barrel. Many of his "students" were already practiced in the art of gunfighting, but in Harry's view they were all beginners.

Each day he would have them shoot at still targets, moving targets, at bottles, playing cards, poker chips. One day he set up two lucifers on a corral pole and shot each, lighting each into a flame— separately.

Hamp Hampton, viewing it from inside the barn, called it "mighty fine pistoleering." His son Miles, standing next to him, was as impressed with Harry Poon's shooting as he was with Old Hamp's command of the English vocabulary. He'd never heard that word before—pistoleering—but he knew he'd never forget it.

On rainy days Harry took them inside the barn, which wasn't as much fun, but it killed time. Gunfighters always seemed to have time on their hands, and perhaps that was one of the reasons they sometimes appeared so zealous in the pursuit of trouble. At least, that was a notion forwarded by Dr. Golightly in one of his conversations with John Slocum.

"They are bored; that's what the trouble is. And, by jingo, when those six or whatever number gunmen out there with Hamp Hampton and his boys get real bored enough they'll blow their wickey."

"I do believe you," Slocum said. "What do you recommend as medicine for it, Doc?" And he watched a fly buzzing at the windowpane in Doc's office.

"I don't know what to recommend, young feller,

but I do feel it is time for you to make your play—
if you aim to make a play, that is," he added.

Slocum had been hunkered down alongside the
door while Doc put his tools away, having finished
his final examination of his patient's gun wound.

Now he rose to his feet, took his hat off his head,
set it again at a different angle, and hitched up his
pants.

"I believe you're right, Doc." And he nodded,
touched the brim of his hat with his thumb, and left
the office. The visit had taken no more than half
an hour. Slocum had had a few questions about
Barney Ziegler to throw at Golightly, and some on
the Ellingers and Hamptons, all of which he was
happy to say clarified the picture.

When he reached Jack Creek the sun was just
slipping in back of the range of the Absarokas, and
a slight chill was in the air. It gave him a turn to
see the thin pencil of smoke coming from the cabin.
And when he saw Sally and Billy Ellinger, he fit
the last detail into his plan of action.

He thought she had never looked so fresh, and the
moment she turned to greet him he felt her reaching
out and his own.

"I hope it was all right for us to come," she said.
"Cole sent someone to tell us we'd really better
come on over to his place. But I thought here would
be best. We're closer to the Double E. And Billy
wanted to come here."

"I've always known your brother to have good
sense," he said with a grin. He could hear the boy
cutting up firewood somewhere in the timber.

Her laugh was good to hear. She was wearing a calico dress that he especially liked—loose, but still showing the softness of her full figure. He had stripped his horse in the corral and now as they walked around to the door of the cabin he could hardly tear his eyes from the sharp curve of her quivering breasts.

They had made themselves at home in the cabin, bringing a rug to spread on the dirt floor of the single room. And they had brought supplies.

"Will you take some coffee?"

He was standing in the middle of the room sniffing, a big smile on his face.

"And—uh—some baking-powder biscuits?"

"Can't drink coffee without," he said.

While she brought the coffee and biscuits he seated himself on an empty keg, there being only one chair, which he was leaving for her.

"Still no chance of the Hamptons going through Ten Fork, I reckon," Slocum said.

A sigh ran through her as she came toward him with the mug of coffee. "They're just finishing branding the new calves now. It will be any day."

"There hasn't been any more . . . trouble." And he nodded in the direction of the woodchopping which came indistinctly through the log walls now. "Billy's all right?"

"No trouble. And, yes, he's fine. Just impatient that I won't let him go on over and beat up those boys."

He looked around the cabin, and he knew she was reading his thoughts.

"I'll bed down outside," he said.

"We don't want to put you out."

"You're not putting me out. I've been sleeping outside anyway. Good not to be where visitors expect you. And I can be more able to move when I need to."

"Well, people do know about this place, as we saw the other day when those Ziegler men came."

"At least you'll be out of the way of the drive."

He had put down his coffee and as she turned from the jumbo stove he rose and took a step toward her.

"Not now," she said. "Billy might come in."

"I wasn't figuring on now."

She bit her lip. "Of course. I know you weren't. I'll find you later. Come on, let's have our coffee."

And there was that little smile that he liked so much, while she lowered her head as she so often did when venturing a point.

It was for him one of her delights, the way she spoke. Her voice was soft, yet with a slight counter current in it; as in a stream of water there is often a second, contrary current which, while appearing to be against the main stream, is nevertheless complementary. In the same manner, the slight grain that came into her voice now and again made a setting for the soft, musical quality, which by itself wouldn't have been as interesting.

There were a number of such singular and almost hidden details about her: the way she spoke, her movement, the manner in which she listened. It was, he decided, as though she had never imitated anyone, had never been taught, and had her own unique qualities and special atmosphere.

There was a sudden crash outside as Billy dropped a load of kindling onto the stack by the door. In a moment he came clomping in, preceded by his enormous hat and flying yellow hair.

"Saw your horse outside, Slocum!"

"Pretty good eyesight you got there, son."

"Haw!"

"Billy . . . we'll be having dinner soon. You've got all your chores done?"

"All done." He had hunkered down on his heels, twirling the blade of grass between his fingers, while holding the other end in his mouth; his eyes centered on Slocum.

Slocum was glad to see that the boy had recovered from his fight. His eye was normal, with only a faint discoloration showing above it, and his hand, about which he knew Sally had worried, appeared to be back to what it had been.

To Slocum he seemed quieter, but no less secure. Was it that he was suddenly older? He found himself wondering what would become of the two of them, wondering if Burt Hampton had been around.

"What have you done with your cattle?" he asked, not wanting his thoughts to drift idly.

"They're with the rest of the Ellinger stock," Sally said. "I guess we'll both help when it's time to move them to summer range."

"Did you used to go by Ten Fork, too?"

"Yes. We all did. But then things were different. Barney Ziegler was more friendly. Now he claims he needs that range for his own cows."

"But you won't have to go the long way around, like the Hamptons."

"That's right," Billy said, cutting in fast. "Exceptin' the Hamptons claim they're gonna bust right through the Double E and not take all that time and expense going around."

"Billy, Slocum knows all that already."

She had started to lay the table for their meal, and Slocum watched her while his thoughts ran over the situation again. Well, there was one card he could play. He didn't think it had much chance, but something had to be done.

"I've got something I've got to do," he said, getting to his feet. "I better get to it."

She didn't show her disappointment, and her expression of simple acceptance was still before his eyes as he rode out on the spotted pony.

Not even Hamp knew Old Crouch's age. He wouldn't have cared anyway. And for sure the rusty old dog didn't give a damn for such civilized nonsense as age. Right now he was sleeping. The sun was hot; the ground upon which he lay outside the cabin door was ticking with heat. The dog was sleeping, but not wholly asleep. Hamp was inside the cabin, and where Hamp was, there was Crouch. The muscle just above his left eye, around which there was a black ring of fur, twitched, but his eyes remained closed. Like any surviving animal or man on the frontier, Old Crouch knew how to sleep half awake. He lay on the ground there as though he had been poured onto it, as though he was part of the terrain. Around Crouch no flies buzzed. His owner had pointed out that they wouldn't have dared.

Crouch suddenly lifted his head, his old eyes

bent toward the long draw leading down to Goose
Creek. A growl collected in his throat, but he didn't
bark. He was not Hamp Hampton's dog for nothing.
The growl was all that was necessary, and a bark
would have been heard down by the creek.

Hamp heard him. He had been dozing at cards
with his boys, having partaken liberally of whiskey.
Now, laying down hs hand, he rose, sniffing,
scratching, went to the south porthole, and looked
out.

"Gimme them glasses," he said without looking
back into the cabin.

"What you see, Hamp?"

The old man took the glasses Burt handed him
and peered through, adjusting the lenses.

Crouch gave another little growl outside and now
raised up on his two front legs.

"I heard you, boy," the old man said. He was
chewing vigorously as he studied the land below.

"What you see?" Clyde asked from the table.

"Well, it ain't no naked lady, by God!"

His three sons watched his back as his shoulders
started to shake, and at last a cackle emerged from
his sparsely toothed mouth. "We have got company."

He put down the glasses and turned to face his
three offspring.

"Guess who?"

"Ellinger."

"Clyde, you tell 'em in the bunkhouse. And get
Poon and Hammerhead. They'll stay outta sight."

"It is Ellinger?" Burt asked.

"It is Slocum," Hamp Hampton said. "And you

dumb shits had best mind your P's and Q's. I will do the talking." His eyes opened large as he looked directly at Burt. "You 'specially. You watch yerself. He is no man to mess with. I will see what he wants."

"Why don't we just drop him. Shoot the son of a bitch and drop him in the river. Nobody'll miss him." Burt said the words quickly, in a hurry to get them all out before Hamp cut him off.

A chuckle rose from the wrinkled throat now, and came gargling out of Hamp's mouth, which he had made very round, like a funnel. "Nobody'll miss Slocum? I'll miss him, by God!" Suddenly he straightened. "Now stop all this funnin'. I made a deal with Poon. You leave Slocum, by God, or you'll have to answer to Poon. And—and by God to me!" He spat swiftly onto the dirt floor of the cabin as Clyde went out the door, then whistled, bringing Crouch inside.

"Crouch saw him. Why didn't one of them jack-anapes outriders see him, God damnit!"

The outriders had seen him; it was just that Crouch had been quicker. Slocum spotted one of them riding back to report his entry into the Hampton domain.

He kept his eyes straight ahead, not allowing his attention to be taken, but seeing ahead and in the wide periphery of his vision, keeping his eyes soft, receptive. And, of course, there wasn't only Hamp and his boys and their gunmen and other relatives; there was Harry Poon and that bugger who'd shot

him. It was sure stiffer than riding in on Barney
Ziegler.

And all at once he remembered Old Hill. Hill
had been part Cherokee, part white, and, some said,
all poison. But he was a tough man, telling Slocum
once: "Fact is, boy, a man can't live forever. Not
even in this here country." Well, he thought, as he
rode closer to the Double H buildings, Hill was
right. You can't live forever. And he had always
liked that thought. He liked it right now, as he
loosened more in his saddle and began to whistle
a ditty between his teeth as he rode closer to whatever was waiting for him.

He rode right up to the biggest cabin and as he
did so he felt around him. Drawing rein, he didn't
look about, but sat his horse, calling out, "All right,
boys. You can come on out. I ain't going to hurt
you."

"Jesus H. Christ!" muttered Hamp Hampton.
"That son of a bitch has got harder balls than a
brass monkey!" With a wicked grin on his face, he
opened the door and walked out to face his visitor.

"Come in and set, Mr. Slocum."

Slocum sat his horse and looked down at Crouch
sniffing around the animal.

"Sure," he said. Dismounting, his eyes swept
the corral, the other ranch buildings, seeing nothing
other than Hamp and his boys.

Inside, he took the chair that was proffered and
refused a drink.

"Had a little more than necessary last night," he
said pleasantly.

Old Hamp chuckled.

"You're the one staying out at the Double E, I am told," Burt burst out suddenly.

"Burt..." The warning came from his brother Clyde.

Slocum looked across the table at Burt Hampton. "You want to make something of that?"

"Burt meant no offense, Slocum," Hamp put in, weaving his gnarled hands through the air in front of him in an effort at placating his visitor.

"I reckon he can speak for himself," Slocum said, not taking his eyes off Burt Hampton, holding his eyes right on until Burt looked away.

"Backwatered you, by God, you puppy!" chuckled Hamp. He grinned at Slocum. "What can I do for you, Mr. Slocum?"

"I'd like you to consider taking your herd through Ten Fork instead of the Double E. I'm here as a friend of the family." His eyes turned cold on Burt Hampton, who once again looked away.

"Can't do that. Barney Ziegler's right-of-way there; that's his'n, and whilst in the past he has permitted us to go that way, he ain't now. Says he needs the graze for his own stock and don't want it being chewed up with all them beeves coming through."

"You ever think of paying him for going through there?"

"Never had to, and I ain't aiming to now."

"And if you go by Horsehead?"

"That takes too long, wears down the cattle, and eats up expense on the drovers. That answer your question?"

Slocum looked slowly at the old man. "Why don't you think it over," he said, "without getting your ass in such an uproar?"

A quick grin sliced across Hamp's face, and one of his sons—Clyde—started to laugh, but caught himself.

"Nothing to think about."

"They got a bank over to Tensleep—that right?"

"I believe that is so," Hamp said carefully, studying it now, his eyes shrewd with thought.

"Might be something could be worked out with Cole, like a loan, something like that—"

"Shit damn it, Hamp!" The words burst from Burt Hampton.

"Shut up!" his father said. "The man is talking money." His attention was fully on Slocum now. "You are talking money to pay Ziegler to let us take the herd through Ten Fork."

"That's what I am saying."

"And I am saying my patience has been run out to the end of my rope. Those ornery Ellingers, they don't listen to no kind of reason! And me for one am not paying a fucking cent to Ziegler or anybody else!"

"Is there any way I can get you to not take your herd through the Double E?"

"There is. You can bring me Cole Ellinger in a pine box."

Slocum put his hands on his knees and stood up. "All right, then."

He looked down at Hamp Hampton, who was sucking his gums and sniffing. Something seemed to be on the old man's mind. Something was.

"You made mention of a bank loan. That's money you're talking about."

"So . . ."

"So I ain't hard to do business with, Slocum. I can take to money. I don't need it, you understand, I don't need it; but if you and the Ellingers could come up with some money and . . . Well, I might— I am saying I *might* consider taking my herd through Horsehead. I mean, you'll be paying *me!*"

"I see."

"But you better study that pretty quick. Spring's a-poppin' and that herd is about ready to move." And he looked right center at Slocum, with the tip of his tongue coming just a little way out of the side of his mouth.

Slocum looked at the three sons of Hamp Hampton, all looking as though they'd had the wind knocked out of them.

"I will talk it over with Cole Ellinger," he said, and with a nod at Hamp, but ignoring his boys, he turned and left the cabin.

As he turned the pony and started back down the long draw he glanced over at one of the other cabins, probably the bunkhouse. He was sure he saw a face in the window. He was sure it was Harry Poon.

Young Billy had not given up on the light in his young heart, but he hadn't seen her since the day he'd pointed out her grandpa slapping his running iron on those beeves down by Willow Creek. And then one day, while he was riding out checking the Double E stock he saw the blue roan horse with the

flaxen mane and the brown hair of its rider, and his
heart jumped.

She was as glad to see him. He could tell. Billy
was a quiet boy, but he wasn't more than a little
shy. It wouldn't be long before he knew who he
was. Slocum thought he did already, and had even
said so to Sally.

Now the boy and girl sat their ponies, looking
out over the great green and brown valley of the
Greybull, with the snow-capped mountains high
above them and the giant rimrocks frowning down.
The day was as clear as a brand-new coin. Billy
listened to a woodpecker pounding into a dead tree.
And he could smell the fresh young scent of the
girl on the horse beside him. It was warm, with the
light lancing through the branches of the willows.

Across from them on the other side of the valley
stretched Manacle Ridge, looking like a razorback
on some huge stone animal.

"How you been?" he asked.

"Good. How you been?"

"Good."

He was chewing on the blade of grass and when
he turned his head toward her the springing end
with the seeds brushed her face. They both laughed.

"Look," he said suddenly. "What's that?" and he
pointed.

"Where?" She was leaning out of her saddle. "I
don't see anything."

"Along the ridge there. Something white or grey.
See it moving?"

"It's like snow, except there isn't any snow," she
said. "I see it now, coming right into the Basin."

"Holy smokes!" Billy Ellinger exclaimed. "Know what it is?"

"What is it?"

"I think it's sheep."

They sat their horses, looking down at the big grey carpet as it flowed over the top of Manacle Ridge and down into Sunshine Basin.

"That's cattle range there," Billy told her.

"That's what I know."

"I sure don't know what those woolies are doing there. They ain't supposed to come this side of the Ridge."

He pulled his horse's head round. "I wonder if they've seen them."

"I don't know how they couldn't," Nan said.

"It'll mean trouble." And then he was sorry he had said it. "Seems something's always happening to spoil it when we meet."

She looked at him. "It isn't spoiled," she said.

"No, that's right. It isn't. Come on. I'll race you over to the butte."

And in the next instant they were racing their horses neck and neck to the big butte almost a half mile away.

Billy knew that he had to win, because he knew what prize he would claim. He was a nervy boy, but he wondered if he really would have the nerve to ask her for a kiss.

# 8

Slocum knew it was in the detail that you really saw what was going on. He knew the value of listening and watching so carefully that you weren't taken by the drama. Riding back from the Double H and his meeting with Hamp Hampton and his boys, his thoughts dwelt on all that he had seen and heard.

He knew that Hamp had no intention whatever of settling his dispute with the Ellingers; he had known it even before he'd ridden out to the ranch. But he had decided what he was going to do and so he had wanted to see these participants in the Sunshine Basin action and also to see if Harry Poon was about.

He had posed the question of money and peace in the Basin to see old Hamp's reaction, not to mention that of his three boys. Slocum was able to catch an indication of Hamp's way—as he had with Barney Ziegler—at least get a feeling of the general way Hamp was. He would stall, pretend to go along with the possibility of a settlement, and then doublecross. No doubt about it, the Hamptons wanted blood, not money, and for sure not talk.

And Barney Ziegler? His thoughts turned to the man in the wheelchair. Ziegler was ready to act, too, but from a different place. A man like Hamp Hampton wanted fun, excitement, thrills, but Ziegler wanted power; Ziegler loved to manipulate people. Barney Ziegler had to have his own way. Always. Felicia was no different—only bending to Ziegler so she could eventually get what she wanted. And to both of them Slocum had done the unpardonable. He had spurned each.

For a moment or so his thoughts dwelt on the time spent with the woman who was Barney Ziegler's wife, at least on paper—the time he had spent with her on her picnic blanket not very long ago. Hunger for her suddenly swept over him, but he pulled himself out of it as he saw again her face tight with the triumph she had found for herself in the encounter. Her triumph was really her defeat, he realized. Yes, she was surely the same as Barney Ziegler in the essentials.

He rode quickly now, as the light from the sun began to lengthen into mid-afternoon. While his instincts were still keened to his surroundings, his thoughts could at the same time work on the question that was struggling in his mind. He knew that while it was necessary to give the situation keen thought, it was action that counted after all. In other words, to have a plan, and at the same time be free enough to improvise and adapt. For instance, where, he asked himself—or who—was the weakest link in the chain of events that was now rushing to a climax in Sunshine Basin?

He had a feeling it wouldn't be long till he found out.


At once he heard the extra silence in the little meadow and as he approached the cabin. He was immediately on special guard, stepping down from his mount well away from the log house and moving in on foot.

He waited in the timber at the edge of the clearing for several moments, feeling the sense of emptiness within the cabin. The corral was empty. There was a good stack of firewood by the front door. He walked around in the timberline checking the cabin from all sides. Then he went up to the front door and entered.

The note on the jumbo stove said simply that they had gone back to the Double E; she knew she belonged there at this time—both of them belonged there.

Slocum could agree with that, though he wished for their safety and knew they were asking for trouble. He didn't waste any time, but only waited for his horse to finish the grain he had put out for him. Then he mounted and headed down to the Double E.

As he rode down the thin trail that led into the small valley between the hills, with the ranch house and corral at the far end, he felt the cool of the early evening on his hands and face. The evening star was just visible and the sky was silent.

There were no cattle about, he noted; he supposed that Cole or the other Ellingers had taken the herd to a safer place. In a few moments he spotted her dun pony and Billy's strawberry roan in the bunch grass on the west side of the cabin. The roan looked up and saw the man and horse approaching, then dropped his head and continued to eat. The dun lifted its head then, kicked at something— maybe a fly on its stomach—shook its head, its mane flying, and let go a low nicker.

Slocum sat his horse and listened. He could hear nothing coming from the cabin. Yet he felt uneasy. The light was leaving the sky, with the sun almost at the horizon. He kicked the spotted horse forward and rode right up to the rear of the cabin and dismounted, dropping the reins to the ground. Drawing his Colt, he stepped to the back door. It was not locked. He took a moment to turn the handle quietly, opened the door, and stepped into the kitchen.

There wasn't a sound in the house and he knew something was wrong, but he had to act. He knew that whoever was there had to have heard him. Stepping quickly through the kitchen, he entered the front room.

Billy cried, "Watch out!"

But his warning was too late. Slocum was already in the room facing Burt Hampton and Sally Ellinger. Burt was holding her from behind with his forearm tight across her neck, cutting off her breath as she kicked and struggled to get free.

"Drop yer gun, Slocum!"

Slocum's Colt Peacemaker fell to the floor. Hampton had his own gun pressed into Sally's ribs, while Billy was standing in the corner of the line of fire.

"Get over there, you son of a bitch!" Hampton flung the girl from him and stood free as she almost fell into Billy. Burt Hampton covered the three of them now as he waved Slocum closer to the Ellingers with his gun barrel.

"By God! What luck! You came to me! Hell, I knew you would! I been waiting. Heard all about you, Slocum. Heard all about you messing with my girl here!"

Suddenly Sally sprang forward, but stopped as Hampton brought his gun right in line with her. Her face was flushed, her lips trembling with anger, her eyes stabbing at him as her words broke out. "You stop that talk, Burt Hampton! I am no girl of yours— or anything of yours! Now, I'm telling you again —get out of here! Get out! Get out!"

Her force was so powerful that even though Burt Hampton was holding his gun on her he had to take a step back. But then his thin face, which was the color of butcher paper, slid into a smile. "Why so unsociable, Sal? I only just got here. Been aiming to come by and see you. I missed you! Didn't know your . . . uh . . . friend there would be along too. Hell, he was just up at the Double H. Must of read my mind and hightailed it right back here to see ya!" He grinned. He had two teeth missing, in the front row. His lips were wet, his little eyes red and creamy. "Figured it, Slocum! Figured you'd come lollygag-

gin' after some of that real good stuff, by God!"
And he threw back his head and laughed.

In that split second Burt Hampton's mirth was
his undoing. Slocum took one step forward and
kicked him right in the kneecap. Burt screamed,
his gun exploded, the bullet plunging harmlessly
into the floor.

In the echo of his scream of pain Slocum slammed
him in the neck with a powerhouse left, followed
by a right in the diaphragm. Burt's breath barked
out of him as he bent double in total agony. It was
not necessary, but Slocum had to do it for the three
of them. He brought his right around in a chopping
punch on the side of Burt Hampton's jaw. The
youngest of Hamp Hampton's sons fell to the floor
as though poleaxed.

It was Burt Hampton who broke the long silence,
stirring and muttering on the floor as he began to
regain consciousness.

Slocum watched him carefully, and as the fallen
man drew up an arm and a leg, he said, "Get out!
Don't ever come back."

The defeated man rose to his feet, staggered a
little, then gained control of himself. He was bloody;
his face was hideous with pain and fury. Sally turned
away, and with a muffled sound hurried into the
next room. Billy remained, his jaw fallen open in
awe. Only Slocum held the measure of the moment.

"Get out," he said again.

Burt Hampton's words rasped out of his short
throat. "I'll be back, Slocum. The Hamptons will
be back, God damn you!"

Still staggering slightly, he made his way to the door, opened it, and went out. Through the window Slocum watched him walking to the edge of a stand of spruce. In another moment or two he led his saddle horse out, mounted painfully, and rode away.

When Sally came back into the room she said, "He came just before you got here. He... he was ... foul!" Her eyes filled with tears of indignation and hurt. She turned to Billy. "You all right, mister?"

"Uh-huh." The boy was pale.

"You're a lucky boy, son," Slocum said, "with a sister like that."

Billy didn't say anything.

That night Slocum slept outside the house in the timber surrounding the little valley. He slept fully clothed, with his Colt Peacemaker in his hand, half awake; even in his near-sleep he felt the sounds, smelled the changing odors of the night. Twice he awakened fully, at the bark of a coyote. Then, after listening, he decided it was animal and not man. And once, deep into the night, he rose and walked the few steps to the edge of the timber to look down at the house. All seemed well, but he did not relax his vigilance, even so. He slept again, in that special border place of half-awake, half-asleep where he could, as it were, listen to both worlds. In the predawn he awakened fully, rolled his bedding, and walked back down to the house.

They had finished breakfast when they heard the horses. Stepping fast to the window, Slocum spoke over his shoulder. "It's Cole and three men."

The visitors rode right up to the front of the cabin

and swung out of their saddles. Slocum opened the door and faced them, with Sally and Billy directly behind him.

"Come in," he said.

Cole, his face tight as dried leather, his grey eyes cutting like flint, nodded, then turned back to his companions, saying, "Put 'em in the barn, boys. Then come on in."

Even before he sat down, his words were falling dramatically into the room. "Barney Ziegler has opened up the Ten Fork to Herkimer and his woolies. We're in for it now!"

He took his hat off and put it on again, his eyes on his niece and nephew. "Damn it, Sal, I figured you were long gone from here, out of this."

"It's our home," Sally said simply.

"I suppose the Hamptons know about the sheep," Slocum said.

Billy, his jaws working fast on a short stem of grass, moved to the table where the men were sitting, while Sally brought coffee.

"I seen them," he said. "I seen them coming over Manacle Ridge."

"Seen them!" Cole stared at the boy.

"Billy, why didn't you tell us?" Sally had stopped in the middle of the room with the coffee pot and sugar bowl in her hands.

The boy's face was suddenly drenched in red embarrassment. "I forgot."

There was a moment of silence, and then quickly Slocum said, "How many were there? How many do you figure?"

"A whole lot. They covered that south slope

between Piney Creek and the big double cutbank."

"That has for sure torn it," Cole said, looking down into his coffee, as Sam and Roy Ellinger walked in. Looking up at them, Cole asked, "Tod?"

"He stopped off," Roy said, with a glance toward Sally's back as she left the room for more cups. "He'll come directly."

When Sally was out of the room, Slocum quickly told them of Burt Hampton's visit.

"Well, we can expect something," Roy Ellinger said wryly.

"You come right over from your place?" Slocum asked as the girl came back into the room, and he raised his voice as he looked at Cole.

Cole nodded, and when the door opened to admit Tod Greenough he said, "I sent riders to the rest of the family with the news. I think we'd best collect at my place. What do you think, Slocum?"

"I think the Hamptons will come here. It's better to stay here."

"Why?" Cole almost snapped the word, leaning forward with his long forearms on the table.

"You get all of you bunched in one place, it could be a mistake."

"It'd give us more firepower," Tod Greenough pointed out.

"And also make you a bigger target," Slocum countered. "All bunched like that, he can pin us down. That's a mistake where there's no one left to have learned the lesson," he added.

Cole was eyeing him hard. "What are you figuring, Slocum?"

"Spread out. Like now, get some men into the

timber. Any of you sharpshooters?"

They exchanged glances between themselves.

"No." Slocum answered his own question.

"But I don't see—" Sam Ellinger started to say.

Slocum cut him off. "Cole here offered me a job to ramrod this outfit. I have just accepted." He looked around at their desperate faces, watching them look at Cole for guidance, then one by one turning back to him.

Slocum was again speaking, not doubting their acceptance of him for a minute. There was no other way.

"Which one of you has got the fastest horse?"

Without hesitation, Cole said, "Here."

Slocum's eyes swept the group, settling on Sam Ellinger. "You take Cole's horse. You'll be the messenger; and the getaway if we get in trouble. Picket your animal on the other side of the creek there." He turned to the others. "Meanwhile, get all those other horses out of the barn and into the timber."

Cole nodded. "Let's get to her."

Slocum was already on his feet, standing still, listening.

"Excepting," he said, "we're already too late."

And his words were nearly drowned by the crash of rifle fire and the thudding of bullets into the door and the log walls of the cabin.

"Ellingers! Slocum! Come on out with your guns down and your hands up! I'm giving you three minutes, and then we'll fire the cabin. You goddamn sheep shitters!"

Hamp Hampton was screaming the words.

Slocum had ordered the men to positions inside the cabin. Stationing himself near one of the two front windows, he fired at someone moving in the trees. A man screamed, telling him his shot had been true.

Almost immediately there was the loud drumming of horses and a band of some dozen men swept past the front of the house pouring rifle fire at the window portals and the front door. Nobody inside the cabin was hit, but Cole knocked one man off his horse, while Slocum shot another in the chest, the man sailing to the ground as his terrified horse raced after its companions.

In a moment the horsemen rode back, their bullets driving into the front of the cabin. This time Roy Ellinger got it in his arm. Slocum shot two horses, setting their riders afoot, and Tod Greenough killed a man.

A sudden cry went up from Roy as he was hit again, this time high in the chest. He fell, blood seeping from him.

Now more rifles joined the forces outside, and Hamp Hampton could be heard screaming orders, cursing everybody, whipping his men and himself into a frenzy.

Suddenly the firing stopped, and a strange stillness fell over the scene. Slocum had the men check their guns, count their ammunition.

"Slocum!" It was Hamp calling.

Slocum moved to the side of one of the windows that was beside the door. "Hampton! I want you to let Sally and Billy Ellinger go. This fight has nothing to do with them."

There was a short silence, then Burt Hampton's voice screamed out, "Like hell it hasn't! We're wiping you all out, Slocum! I'm gonna drink your blood!"

"Shut up, you asshole!" roared his father. "God damn it, shut your mouth! You have caused enough trouble already. You speak any more and I am going to whip your ass!"

There was a pause after this brisk parental disciplining, then Hamp called out, "Slocum! You hurt my boy, Burt. That means you hurt me! You get that? Now then, you come on out and we will let the girl and the boy go. Otherwise, Hamp Hampton is gonna take you down in little pieces!"

Inside the cabin, Slocum listened carefully to the old man as he stood in the middle of the room reloading the Winchester.

"Slocum, you're not to think of that," Sally said. "I will never agree to that!" She faced him, adamant, a stone wall of intention.

"Sure," he said.

"You know if you do that he'll shoot you right down, and Sal and Billy, too," Cole said. "He wants to wipe out all the Ellingers. He's crazy. The old bastard's crazy!" Cole pushed his fist against Slocum's arm in emphasis. "You can't make any deal with him!"

"That's what I know. But we are not in a good spot here, my friend. We are going to run out of ammo, water, food, and more sooner than later, we're going to run out of each other."

"Slocum . . ." She had grabbed the sleeve of his shirt.

But he only grinned at her and turned away.

"We'll wait on it," he said, looking at the door.

The silence lengthened with the day. Now and again Slocum tried to take a look out one of the windows. Twice bullets ripped into the cabin right by his head.

The long morning was interrupted by sporadic shooting from the Hamptons, by occasional return fire from the cabin. Sally had dressed Roy Ellinger's wounds, but he was in poor shape.

"I believe his lung is hit," Slocum said, speaking low to Cole so that Roy wouldn't hear.

Roy was tough; he didn't utter a word of complaint. He even joked with Sally as she attended him. Tod Greenough had been nicked in the hand; a splinter, knocked out of one of the logs by a Hampton bullet, had narrowly missed Billy's eye, drawing blood along his cheek.

Around noon Hamp Hampton shouted out his offer again, and Slocum told him he was studying on it. His answer was greeted by the old man's curses. But Slocum was waiting. Hamp had another card, and he hadn't dealt it. Where was Harry Poon?

The atmosphere in the cabin was tight. No one was looking forward to the night.

They'll try firing the cabin come nightfall," Sam Ellinger said.

"We have got a long hope," Cole said to Slocum. "Any of the Ellingers who might notice we ain't around could get the wind up and start looking for us."

"Hamp's figured that one, and he'll have an ambush laid out," Slocum replied evenly as he watched the sunlight lengthening through one of the side windows.

"They'll figure on us making a break for it once it's dark," Sam Ellinger said.

A sudden barrage of rifle fire at the front of the house took their attention. Slocum stepped to one of the side windows and began firing at two men pulling the gig away from the side of the barn. When one man dropped, his companion fled.

"They're aiming to fill the gig with brush and fire it and roll it into the door," he warned. He ordered Billy to keep a watch on it.

Cole Ellinger lowered his rifle and stepped away from the window. "It'll be dark soon."

"About time me and Hamp had a talk," Slocum said.

"Talk!" Cole stared at him as though not believing what he'd heard. "What the hell you going to talk about? The minute you step out there, you're dead!"

"We have got a card out there in that pack of gunfighters," Slocum said.

They had moved to one corner of the room so that the others couldn't hear them. From where he was standing, Slocum could see Sally through the doorway into the kitchen, where she was preparing food for the men. He had a moment, one of those in-between pictures given free, as it were, where he could see a person off-guard, revealing something of his true nature. It was just such an in-between moment when without any intention on his part his eye caught her from the side, standing at the stove with her sleeves rolled up; with the back of her wrist she was brushing the hair away from her face. It was a moment that touched him. And at the same time, he was aware without a drop of sorrow that it could be the last time he would see her.

"So what's this card you're talking about?" Cole was impatient, beginning to lose his famous phlegmatic attitude.

"The card is Harry Poon."

"That gunfighter?"

"There is only one Harry Poon," Slocum said carefully. "And he has traveled a long, long way and gone to one hell of a lot of trouble to build yours truly a pine box. And I'd bet right into anybody's fistful of aces that Mr. Poon wants—and more than likely is demanding—to have the pleasure for his own sweet self."

"You're figuring how to arrange your own funeral, that it?" Cole's tone was sour.

Slocum canted his head as he squinted at Cole Ellinger. "Mr. Ellinger, you hired me to do a job, and I am aiming to do it. That is, I am aiming to whipsaw this little how-de-do and outsmart and outgun that old man out there and that spinny-stick gunfighter and his sidekick who on purpose didn't kill me on that mountain but saved me for Harry. And I do not need your smart-ass remarks, so get your ass to that window and cover me!" And he grinned at Cole Ellinger, the head of the Ellinger clan, totally disarming him, so that Cole almost laughed back, and felt himself loose again.

"I am ready," Cole said. And then he repeated what he had said before. "It'll be getting dark soon."

"It'll be just as dark for them as it will be for us."

"Slocum, you're not really..." Cole started to say, and then he remembered and stopped, saying, "Never mind it."

"Slocum!" It was Hamp, seeming closer somehow, though they could see he was still concealed within the line of shrubbery at the trees that gave protection to the Hampton forces.

"Slocum, you still want us to let the girl and boy go? It's coming dark directly, and we're going to fire the cabin. You come on out and we'll let 'em go."

"For heaven's sake..." Sally was standing beside him now, her hand to her mouth, unable to go on.

But Slocum wasn't listening to her. He was listening outside the cabin. Waiting. And now what he had been waiting for was there as a new voice came in, one he hadn't heard in a while, but which he had no trouble recognizing.

"Slocum, I am waiting for you!"

It was what he'd been waiting for. He nodded to Cole. "That's Poon. You locate where he is; listen to him. I'll get him to talk."

"Poon," he called out. "Come on out in front of the cabin and fight me fair. Then we'll let the Ellingers and Hamptons settle their own."

There followed a silence then. And he knew Harry Poon was weighing it.

"He's just setting you up for crossfire," Cole said.

"You and me, Slocum?" Poon called.

And in the cabin Slocum looked at Cole Ellinger and pointed in the direction where Harry Poon's voice was coming from.

Instinctively, he was placing himself in the gunfighter's thoughts. Would Harry try the same thing again, as he had on the mountain? Would he have his accomplice, the man on the trail who'd shot Slocum, hidden away now, cutting him down in crossfire, but only wounding him so that Harry—not so sure of himself any more, what with consumption and age—could deliver the big killing? It was a bold thought, but it fit. It fit tighter than stretched cowhide on a set of saddle panniers. It had to be that. It had to be! It was Harry Poon's great big picture of himself as the West's greatest gunfighter ever. It was what had caught him at Jicarilla Bob's in Forth Worth, and it might be just what would catch him now. The important thing was to figure where the other man would be firing from, not to mention the fact that he would only wound him, and not too badly. Because Harry Poon had to look good. Harry Poon had to win the big one.

And Hamp, he suddenly thought. Would Hamp stand for it? Would he let Harry pull it off? Why not? Hamp didn't care a damn about him, Slocum; he wanted the Ellingers.

Slocum took his hat off and adjusted it a little more closely on his head. By God, he was thinking; by God, he was going to have to slip quicker than a silk snake.

# 9

"I am ready, Slocum!"

Slocum took a quick look out the window. There was nobody in sight. He checked the Colt, and then slipped a second handgun which he usually carried in his bag into his shirt, tying it around himself with a leather thong so that it held flat and in position.

"Slocum!"

He checked again the direction of the voice, nodding to Cole. Good, the bushwhacker would hit him from the left, and Harry Poon would come at him from the right.

"Sam, open the door. Everybody ready now!"

As the door opened a cool breeze swept in, and for an instant he heard the flutter of leaves in the trees. But only for a second; he hardly noticed it.

Every grain of his attention was now only on what was taking place with the desperate man who was waiting for him.

"All right, Harry, let me see you!"

"The pleasure will be mine, Slocum. For indeed, 'The world's an inn and death the journey's end.' Eh, Slocum?"

Stepping out, he looked quickly with his side vision toward the voice, but Poon was still hidden. The bushwhacker could be anywhere, he knew. He had reckoned on him coming from his left; but the shot came neither from right nor left, but from where Harry Poon had called out to him. Slocum felt the slug strike off his left arm, a slight glance, but enough to startle if he hadn't been prepared for it; he spun under the impact, but didn't fall.

"Slocum!"

There was Harry Poon—thin, angular, his face the color of candle wax behind that black mustache. And Slocum was now dropping, dropping intentionally, rolling as he hit the ground. Harry Poon's shot went harmlessly through the air where a split second before Slocum had been standing. In one flowing movement Slocum brought the Colt up and fired. He kept on rolling right on up to his feet, seeing Harry Poon drop from the bullet that had taken him through both lungs. Then he was firing at the big, red-faced man who had stepped out from the trees where Poon had been. Yes, he had miscalculated. But he'd got Harry Poon, and now there was the bushwhacker. His gun suddenly fell from his hand and he realized that the other man's bullet had knocked it out of his grip. Within the space of a breath, Slocum had reached into his shirt and drawn his second gun. Under the impact of his swift bullet the big man with all the red hair went down like a foundering buffalo, emptying his own hand-gun nowhere as Slocum shot him right between the eyes.

Meanwhile, guns were firing all around him as the Ellingers broke from the cabin. As he raced for the trees, watching for Sally and Billy so that he could cover them, he felt rather than saw the horse bearing down on him from behind. Instinct turned him aside as the rifle barrel smashed down where his head would have been, but now caught his shoulder, almost knocking him down, causing him to drop his handgun.

It was Burt Hampton, turning his horse and ready to charge him again. The firing had suddenly stopped. It was a strange moment. All that could be heard was the panting of the horse and the drumming of its hooves on the ground. For a moment it felt to Slocum as if everything had stopped.

Then two rifle shots broke that stillness. He watched Burt Hampton straighten up in his saddle as his horse galloped on. As Slocum jumped out of the way, Burt Hampton fell at his feet.

Slocum looked down at the dead man. He heard Cole Ellinger shouting, "You men had enough? I have shot Hamp Hampton! Have the rest of you had enough?"

The silence that fell upon those words seemed all there was. There was nothing left. Only the silence and the dead. And young Billy Ellinger looking at the body of Burt Hampton, the first man he had ever killed.

The last wisp of gunsmoke had vanished from the scene of battle. The angry guns were holstered. It was time to bury the dead, to take care of the wounded. Roy Ellinger had cashed in, and this was considered a mercy. Tod Greenough had taken a bad one in the thigh, but not mortal. Burt Hampton was dead, and two Hampton gunmen, plus Harry Poon and Hammerhead Hogan.

To everyone's surprise on both sides, Hamp Hampton was still alive.

"I thought I'd killed the son of a bitch," Cole grumbled to Slocum as the old man was carried into the Double E house.

Doc Golightly had been sent for. He had been found at a neighboring ranch, and so wasn't long in coming.

"You'll live," he told the oldest Hampton.

"Too mean to die is what you're saying, ain't it, Golightly?"

Doc chuckled, looking down at his patient, who was lying on Sally Ellinger's horsehair sofa.

"But poor Burt is dead," the old man went on. "I still got Clyde and Miles. I will say, Burt asked for it." He held up his hand to stay comment from those who were gathered around him. "I am holding no grudge, on account of what Slocum has just told me, and I know it's the God's own truth. That son of a bitch Barney Ziegler has been hell-bent on wiping all of us off the face of the earth. Wants to take over Sunshine Basin. I have knowed it this good while! By God, if he ever does that, it'll be over some dead body, and it will not be mine!"

The old man was back in form as his bent for warfare and intrigue resumed in a fresh direction. "Cole, soon as I'm about—tomorrer, likely—we'll have us a powwow on how we'll handle that son of a bitch."

Suddenly his eyes closed, his face screwing tight in what appeared to be concentration.

"You all right, Hamp?" It was Clyde, bent over his father with concern.

The eyes opened, tears of uncontrollable mirth springing from them, and laughter rattled out of his wet lips. "Just recollecting how I run into Barney Ziegler and Clarence Herkimer not so un-recently down to Sister Ellie's . . ." The mouth opened wider as a fresh cackle sprang forth, round and lively as a brand-new egg. "Dippin' their wicks, by jingo! And Barney with that luscious little piece he's got back home. Man's got to be crazy going to Sister's when he's got the likes of that any time he gets a notion!"

Reaching down, he began rooting in his enormous pants.

"What's the matter, Hamp?" Doc Golightly, bronze eyes pink from overindulgence in booze the night before, bent solicitously to his patient.

"Christ, I can't find my whanger in these goddamn over-halls, and I know I still got it here somewheres. Least that's what I hope . . . !" And he roared at his own wit, and those around him joined in.

"Got to scratch it once in a while, 'specially with

them goddamn fleas we got back home. You boys—
Clyde, you and Miles, now—with Burt gone, you
get rid of them fuckin' fleas. Clean that cabin. Get
rid of them things!"

"Those fleas are likely from Old Crouch," Miles
said. Instantly he realized his error.

The old man almost raised up, but Doc pressed
him gently back onto the couch. "From you, not
from Crouch. That dog is cleaner than any human
I know! Shit, where is Crouch?"

"Back home, Hamp."

"For Christ's sake, somebody get me a drink!"

He droned on, and finally, aided by whiskey, he
fell asleep, his snores rolling out of his strange nose
and down his chest.

Presently the wagon arrived and Doc Golightly
supervised the loading of his patients.

When they were gone Cole Ellinger turned to
Slocum. "You'll come by to see us, Slocum."

"Sure will."

"Where to now?"

"Thought I'd try the Powder River country."

The moon was up and the sky was filled with
stars when the last of them left. Only Slocum and
the two Ellingers remained at the Double E.

Slocum watched her looking about the wreckage.
But it was only a moment, then she began picking
up the mess.

"Why don't you leave that till morning," he said.
"We can sleep outside under the stars."

She smiled at him. Billy wanted to stay in the
house. "They couldn't take our house," he said.

It was a while before his excitement cooled

enough so that he could get to bed. They had talked a bit about the fighting, and Slocum had a private word with the boy about Burt Hampton as they sat together on Billy's bedroll.

"He's fine," he said as he came back to Sally, who was moving furniture around in the front room. "He's all right."

They were silent for a moment, just standing there looking at each other.

"Is there anything you want?" she asked.

"Yes."

"I'll see if he's asleep."

When she came back he took the two blankets she had brought. It was cool in the little meadow, just right for their naked bodies.

When she lay down beside him she said, "I'm kind of glad you're not going to be hanging around."

"I'm disappointed," he said, smiling down at her. "I thought you liked it."

She blew her breath teasingly up into his face. "Slocum, you ought to learn to listen better. I am saying one thing, and you are hearing something else."

He grinned into her ear as he slid his leg over her yearning body and when he slipped his member between her legs she reached down to guide him into her. Wrapped in their exquisite embrace they began to dance their passion, moving slowly at first as they found their single rhythm and moved more quickly, but never, never hurrying. She was already totally open to his massive organ as they swept toward a deeper delving and spreading—and finally, an overwhelming coming.

Later in the night he awakened to feel her lips on his cock which was already stiff as a tree. Sucking him slowly she brought him, as he emptied himself into her throat, while she continued sucking and pumping the base of his cock which she couldn't get all the way into her mouth, and with her other hand squeezing the last drop out of his balls.

He had her again just before dawn, almost hurting her with his great thrusting, and their twin explosion emptied them completely.

He didn't know if she was only pretending to be asleep when he rose and dressed, but if she was pretending he knew that was what she wanted, and if she was really asleep that was for the best, too.

As he rode off he knew it didn't matter where he was heading for next or where he had been. The only thing that mattered at all was to be right where he was right now.